THE WRATH
OF THE
GRINNING
GHOST

THE WRATH OF THE GRINNING GHOST

A JOHNNY DIXON MYSTERY: BOOK TWELVE

BRAD STRICKLAND

BASED ON CHARACTERS BY
JOHN BELLAIRS

OPEN ROAD
INTEGRATED MEDIA
NEW YORK

ISBN 978-1-4976-3780-1

This edition published in 2014 by Open Road Integrated Media, Inc.
345 Hudson Street
New York, NY 10014
www.openroadmedia.com

For Phyllis Fogelman

CHAPTER ONE

The noon sun glittered on a million skipping waves. Beneath Johnny Dixon's bare feet, the deck of the *Swordfish* rose and fell. The engine roared, and the boat's bow sent up a cool, salty spray. Johnny and his father were heading into port now, but their deep-sea fishing boat was still so far out in the Gulf of Mexico that Johnny could see no trace of land.

Johnny leaned against the rail, licked his lips, and tasted salt water. He smiled and squinted at the wide horizon through his sunglasses. He hardly ever wore sunglasses, because he was nearsighted and had to wear regular glasses, but his dad had bought him a nifty pair of dark green clip-ons. They made the whole world look different to Johnny, somehow sharper and more alive than it normally appeared.

Behind him, his father, Major Harrison Dixon, twirled the wheel, and the *Swordfish* made a long curve. Johnny looked back at his dad, and Major Dixon's tanned, craggy face broke into a wide grin. "Enjoying yourself, Old Scout?" said the major.

Johnny nodded and turned back, straining to see the first flat gray smudge of land on the edge of the world. It was a hot June day in the mid-1950's, with a high blue sky, piles of fluffy white clouds drifting by, and a bright, clear sun.

Johnny was a pale, freckled, blond boy of about thirteen. He remembered the first time his dad had taken him deep-sea fishing in Florida. Back then, Johnny had felt terrified as they headed out into the Gulf. He had a strong imagination, and he could picture all sorts of disasters. Their boat could capsize, drowning them. They could run out of fuel and drift helplessly until they starved. Sharks or giant octopuses or even sea monsters might attack.

It took Major Dixon's cheerful competence at the wheel to calm Johnny's fears. After that first queasy day, Johnny loved being out at sea. He never once got seasick, and he relished the feeling of freedom. No roads, no signposts, no landmarks told them where they could go or how fast they could speed in getting there. Major Dixon, who was an Air Force pilot, said it was the next best thing to flying. Johnny had flown in airliners a couple of times, but he thought this was even better, the swoop and dip of clipping the waves. The boat almost breathed beneath his feet, as if it were a living creature.

Suddenly, Johnny straightened, shading his eyes with his hand. Was there something different about the eastern horizon? Yes, he was sure! "Land ho!" he bellowed.

"Where away?" his dad roared, laughing.

"Dead ahead!" responded Johnny. He ducked down into the cramped little cabin and ran back up with his father's ten-power Air Force binoculars. Steadying them on the rail, he swept the distant, shadowy line of land. Most of it was only a faint gray pencil line drawn straight across their path, but in one place an indistinct little point stuck up. "I see the harbor light," he shouted. "It's, um, about five points to starboard!"

"Aye, aye," Major Dixon said, adjusting the wheel again.

Ahead of them, Johnny saw the thin vertical line slide to the left until it lay straight ahead. It looked no larger than the point of a pin, but Johnny knew that it was really the tall white tower of Live Oak Key Lighthouse. It would grow larger and larger until they entered the bay between the sandy island and the mainland. Then they would pass within a few hundred yards of it. There probably would be people fishing in skiffs bobbing all around it, and they would wave and yell out to ask how the tarpon had been running.

Johnny sighed in contentment. It had been a great five days. Tomorrow was the end of the vacation, and he and Major Dixon would return to the mainland. They would take a bus to Tallahassee, where they would board a train. That would take them up the long curve of the Atlantic coastline, through Washington, D.C., and New York City. Finally, nearly a whole day later, they would arrive in Duston Heights, Massachusetts. There Johnny would have more fishing stories to tell to his friends Fergie Ferguson, Sarah Channing, and Professor Roderick Childermass. Major Dixon would stay another day or two before he had to return to his duties in Colorado.

Johnny's mother had died of cancer years before. Then his father, a veteran World War II pilot, had rejoined the Air Force to fly fighter planes in the Korean War. Johnny had moved in with his grandfather and grandmother, who lived on Fillmore Street in Duston Heights, an old manufacturing town north of Boston. When he had first arrived, he had been sunk in grief, but over the years he had come to look on Duston Heights as home. Now he didn't know what he would do without the friendship of the people he had met there.

"Want to steer?" asked Major Dixon.

"Sure!" replied Johnny, scrambling back to the wheel.

"Here you go."

Johnny took the wheel from his dad. It vibrated under his hands as he clenched his fingers around the spokes. He turned the wheel right, and then he turned it back left. That is, he turned it to *starboard* and then to *port,* in ship terms. The *Swordfish* made a long, lazy S curve in response. Johnny's dad had rented the boat for the week. Still, Johnny felt a sense of ownership. He told the boat which way to go with the wheel, and it obediently turned in that direction.

Major Dixon took the binoculars and went forward. "That's fine right there," he said. "We're on exactly the right heading."

Johnny nodded. Whenever his dad let him steer, he always liked to pretend he was at the wheel of a pirate ship. He felt like Tyrone Power or Douglas Fairbanks, Jr., or Errol Flynn. Those were famous movie stars who had made pictures about pirates (*good* pirates) who had fought against evil governors or admirals. Johnny loved to read books about the old-time buccaneers too. Some were fiction, like Robert Louis Stevenson's *Treasure Island*, with its cunning Long John Silver, and Rafael Sabatini's *Captain Blood*. Others were true stories about real pirates like Captain Kidd, Edward Teach (better known as Blackbeard), and Gasparilla.

In fact, Johnny did more than just read about pirates. Lately, he had started a new hobby. He put together wooden models of sailing ships. His first couple hadn't been so great. Their masts sagged and their lines drooped, and the paint jobs were blotched and streaky. As Sarah Channing had observed, they looked like ships a pirate might pity so much that he wouldn't plunder them. He might instead stop and offer to help them, she said. But Johnny was getting better. When he got back home, he planned to start a new model, of the *Hispaniola*, the schooner in which Long John Silver and young Jim Hawkins had sailed to Treasure Island.

He leaned to the right to look ahead. The land was closer now. He could see colors, the hazy yellow-white of sand, the misty gray-green of trees, and here and there the glare of sunlight reflecting from the windows of houses or the sides of cars. The lighthouse began to look like a lighthouse, a tall, tapering tower of white against the darker land and the blue sky. Between the *Swordfish* and the harbor entrance, half a dozen sailboats were tearing along under their triangular white sails.

Major Dixon came clambering back. "Lots of small-craft traffic dead ahead. I'd better take her in, Johnny. You go forward and help me navigate!"

"Sure," said Johnny, giving up the wheel. He took the binoculars and went to the rail again. The major throttled back, so they weren't going so fast. Johnny looked at the sailboats through the binoculars. Many of the people aboard them wore life jackets, as Johnny and his dad did. Some were just in bathing suits.

Johnny turned the binoculars on the Live Oak Key Lighthouse. He swept them up from the base of the tower to the top. For some reason, whenever he looked at the tower, he always felt a peculiar kind of chill. Sometimes he even shivered a little. He didn't know why. He clenched his teeth now, but he still felt his breath coming a little faster and the hair on his arms trying to prickle up.

The tower was clear in the binoculars, its white-painted bricks flaking in places and streaked with rust in others. The gallery—the railed platform that ran around the light chamber at the top—was empty, as always. The light was not on during the day. Gulls swooped around the top of the tower.

And then one of the gulls stopped and just hung in the air, right above the tower dome. It was darker than the other gulls. In fact, Johnny decided, it was black as it hung there against the blue sky. He had never seen a black gull. Puzzled, wondering if it was some kid's kite or something, Johnny tried to focus the binoculars on it.

And then it simply disappeared.

Johnny slowly lowered the binoculars. He swallowed hard. In the pit of his stomach he felt a sinking sensation, as if he were on an elevator that was going down fast. Something was about to happen. He would bet his life on it. He didn't know what it was, but he knew it would not be anything good.

He didn't say anything to his dad about his funny feelings. Major Dixon was a no-nonsense sort of man. It might have been different if Professor Childermass had been along. The professor was short, crabby, and temperamental, but he always listened to anything Johnny had to say, and he would never snort in disbelief. Johnny wasn't sure that his father would be that understanding about something as, well, weird as a vanishing bird. Maybe too, nothing bad would happen. Sometimes Johnny got strange premonitions, and most of the time they did not come true. That was one of the curses of having a good imagination.

Major Dixon slowed the boat even more. They glided right past the base of the lighthouse, which stood on its own small corner of the island. Then Major Dixon turned right. Live Oak Key was what is called a barrier island. It rose from the Gulf of Mexico about a mile from the mainland. Between it and the rest of Florida was a flat, calm stretch of water called Alachamokee Bay. The island itself was home to a community of fishermen, guides, and boat people. They were a cheerful, loud bunch, and they knew the Dixons well.

Johnny heard high fluty calliope music, like a carnival melody. Along the bayside waterfront, he saw people holding on to helium balloons. They were wandering in and out of white canvas tents. The smell of cotton candy drifted across the water, with the sound of laughter.

"What's going on?" Johnny asked as they glided close to the marina where they would tie up their rented boat.

"Don't know," replied his dad. "Looks like some kind of celebration. But I haven't heard anything about it."

They came to the right wharf, and Major Dixon expertly maneuvered the *Swordfish* into its own slip. Johnny jumped up to the wharf, feeling the hot rough wood under his bare feet as he stooped to tie the boat to a cleat with a quick figure-eight knot. Then he ran back to hitch the stern of the boat to another cleat. Major Dixon climbed out and helped him secure the lines.

A tall, skinny, red-faced old man wearing a plaid shirt and a shapeless captain's hat that might have been white a few years before World War I came out of a little booth. He grinned at them with his few remaining teeth. "Welcome back, mateys! Any luck today, Major?"

Major Dixon shook hands with him. "A little, Mr. Weatherall. Johnny and I caught two reasonable-size tarpon. They're on ice now. We won't be able to eat them, so you're welcome to them."

"Right kind of you," Mr. Weatherall said with a beaming smile. "The Missus and I appreciate it."

"Well, let's settle up," Major Dixon said. "By the way, what's going on?"

Mr. Weatherall made a face. It puckered his already wrinkled features until he looked like a shriveled apple. "Aw, this is what they call Pirate Days, Major. A kind o' carnival.

There's games and music and food. It's tourist foolishness." He winked. "Might be fun for a youngun, though."

"Want to go have a look, Johnny?" asked Major Dixon.

"Sure," replied Johnny.

"Get your shoes on and run along, then," his dad told him. "I don't suppose you can get lost on an island! I'll catch up to you as soon as I've paid for the boat and the gas."

Johnny slipped on his boat shoes. They were white canvas with rubber soles, and he wore them without socks. He took off his life jacket and stored it in the big wooden bin beside the marina office. Then he slowly walked down the wharf toward the tents. Lots of people were in costume as pirates, with colorful scarves tied over their hair, big golden hoop earrings, red-and-white striped T-shirts, and even plastic swords at their sides. He saw some carnival games—ringtoss, where you tried to throw wooden rings over the masts of model ships, a dartboard, a shooting gallery where the guns were miniature cannon and the targets were cutouts of pirate ships, and others. Outside one tent, a woman in pirate garb was selling "tattoos." She was just painting them on, but a placard beside her chair showed that they looked like real pirate tattoos: hearts with daggers through them, black Jolly Roger flags with spooky white skulls, mermaids, and lots of other piratey pictures.

Johnny saw a little girl ahead of him lose her grip on a helium balloon. It sailed straight up into the sky. Leaning back to watch it, Johnny thought that now he understood how that strange bird had just vanished. It had probably not been a bird at all. The shape had just been one of these helium balloons that had soared up over the lighthouse and then popped! That was a relief—

"You look like a young man who has many questions."

Johnny almost yelped. He jerked his gaze down from the balloon. A woman stood in front of him. She was very short, no taller than Johnny himself. Her face was wrinkled and as brown as saddle leather. She wore a white turban and a sky-blue dress decorated with embroidered pictures of stars and planets done in silver and gold thread. A brown buckskin belt cinched the dress tight at her waist, and from the belt dangled leather pouches in all colors of the rainbow. The woman's voice had been pleasant, but her face held no expression.

"Uh—hi," said Johnny weakly. "I didn't see you."

The old woman gazed at him. "I sense you have had much to do with the spirits," she said. "I perceive that you are still troubled with many questions. Shall I answer them for you? Twenty-five cents."

Johnny put his hands into the pockets of his cutoff jeans. "I don't have any—" he broke off, feeling something in his right pocket. He pulled it out. It was a shiny silver quarter.

"This way," the woman said, holding open the flap of a white tent. "Don't be afraid. I am not on the side of the shadows."

Holding the quarter, Johnny realized he had no excuse. Despite the woman's reassurances, he couldn't help feeling anxious. With his heart pounding in his throat, Johnny stepped into the tent. When the woman let the flap fall back into place, something odd happened.

All the noise from outside, the music, the laughter, simply faded. It was as if the tent were soundproofed.

A dry, dusty odor filled Johnny's nostrils. His eyes blinked as they adjusted to the dimness. In the center of the tent stood a round table covered with a white silk cloth. A crystal ball the size of a bowling ball was in the very middle of the table. Two straight chairs stood on opposite sides of the ball.

The woman sat in one and held out her hand. "Cross my palm with the silver," she said.

Johnny held out the quarter. He used it to draw an imaginary X in the woman's palm, and then he dropped it into her hand. She closed her fingers on it.

"I am Madam Lumiere," she told him. "The Lady of Light. Be seated, my child."

Johnny sat down on the edge of the other chair. His chest felt squeezed. It was hard to breathe.

Madam Lumiere closed her eyes. "You are not from here,"

she said. "You come from the north. You were born in one place, but you live in another."

Johnny nodded. That was true. He had been born in upstate New York, but now he lived in Massachusetts.

The old woman frowned slightly. "You do not live with your parents," she said. "Your mother is not with you. She has passed over. Your father, ah, your father has duties that take him far away. You live with older people. An aunt? An uncle? No. You stay with a grandfather and a grandmother, no?"

"That's right," said Johnny.

Madam Lumiere's head drooped forward. "I see many strange things in your past," she murmured. "You have done and seen things most people would not believe in. You have an open mind and a brave heart, though you do not know how brave." She opened her eyes. "Something is trying to happen now," she said. "I do not know what. This is very—"

The crystal ball began to glimmer with a peculiar flickering light. It was mostly a pearly white, but there were tinges and flashes of blue. Johnny stared at it, fascinated.

The old woman ran her fingers over the smooth surface of the ball. "Something is coming through, my child," she muttered. "Something very strong, from the other side."

The crystal ball flared with light, like a silent explosion. Johnny saw the light flicker, until a small shape hung in the heart of the crystal. It was a pale white. "What's that?" he asked, his mouth dry.

"I do not know," said Madam Lumiere, her voice sounding troubled. "It is a powerful force—"

Flash! Johnny gasped. The shape had shot out of the crystal ball and hovered above it! It was a face. A dead-white face of a thin man. Long white hair trailed at the sides. The eyes were wide and black. They were the worst of all. The eyes had no whites, no pupils, but were pools as dark and glistening as puddles of oil. Johnny could see no lips on the face, just a gash of a mouth. The creature's mouth opened in a terrible grin.

"Free!" said a dead, rustling voice. "Free! I shall take my

final sacrifice from the world of the living! And the universe shall be mine!"

The monstrous face quivered in the air, and then it vanished. In its place hung something black, the shape of a bird. To Johnny it looked like an eagle or a falcon. It was not flying. The wings were folded, and the figure resembled a statuette of a falcon more than it did a living bird. "Johnny Dixon! Can you hear me?"

The downturned falcon's beak did not move. It couldn't really be speaking, not with any normal voice, but in his head, Johnny heard a raspy voice that was somehow familiar: "Now you've done it! I tried to appear and warn you about what was going to happen, but no! I can't fight this evil thing alone! Get help! Get to Professor Frizz-Face as soon as you can! Or else the world is doomed!"

And then Madam Lumiere shrieked as Johnny toppled out of his chair and fell to the floor.

And everything went dark.

CHAPTER TWO

Johnny heard someone saying, "Child! Child, wake up!" It was a kindly voice, a woman's voice. For a second he even thought it might be the voice of Gramma Dixon.

He opened his eyes. For a dizzy minute he did not know where he was. Everything was dim and shadowy. A wrinkly-faced old woman was bending over him. She held his hand in hers, and he felt her leathery fingers patting the back of his hand. Then it all came back in a rush. Johnny sat up so fast that his head spun. "What happened?"

Madam Lumiere helped him get to his feet. "Easy, easy. You fainted," she said. "You looked into my crystal, saw something, and you fainted dead away. What was it? What did you see?"

Johnny shook his head, trying to clear the mist from his mind. The world seemed to be settling back into place once more. He could smell the dusty tent again, that dry canvas odor, and now he could hear the music and laughter from outside the tent. Whatever strange spell had been hanging over the tent seemed to have gone. "Didn't you see them?" he asked.

"I saw vague, shimmering lights, no brighter than the glow of a five-day-old moon. I heard a humming, as the voice of many hundreds of bees," Madam Lumiere said. "That is all."

Stammering, his words tumbling over one another, Johnny told her of the two things he had seen and heard, of the ghastly pale face and the dark hovering bird.

Madam Lumiere listened gravely. When Johnny finished, she looked deeply concerned. "The first," she said slowly, "the first is a spirit of shadow and malevolence. It may mean you great harm. The second sounds as if it might be a guide, a helper. It could be on your side, offering advice and protection. I cannot tell you more. The rest I think you must learn for yourself. There is great power haunting you, child. You must take care. You must not allow the forces of the darkness to control you." She held up the quarter. "I could return this," she said. "But I will not. What has happened to you is in part my fault. I will keep this and wear it as a charm. Wait a moment."

She reached into a pouch that dangled from her belt. From it she took a large old silver coin. "Take this," she said.

Johnny felt her drop the piece of metal into his hand. It felt strangely heavy. It was only roughly round, and Johnny could see that the engraving on one side showed a cross with small figures inside the spaces between the crosspieces, and the other showed a coat of arms of some sort. Both sides were so very worn that the engraving was hard to make out. "What is it?" he asked.

"A pirate coin," Madam Lumiere told him solemnly. "A *peso de ocho reales*. Marked with the sign of the cross. It has been blessed by a priest, and it has brought luck to men and women of good heart and good soul for more than two hundred years. Keep this with you. When you face danger, think of it. Touch it and think of me too. It may allow me to help you. Go now. Go into the sunlight, but be on guard against the shadows!"

Johnny almost ran out of the tent. His head was spinning. He stepped into the afternoon sunshine and looked around wildly. The hot sun beat down, making his head ache and his eyes water. To Johnny the costumed, happy crowd now looked evil and threatening. The men dressed as pirates leered as if they were eager to feed him to the sharks. He felt like a mouse surrounded by cruel cats, all of them ready to tease him before they began to feast. He felt—

He felt a hand clap down on his shoulder!

"Easy, Johnny!" said his father from behind him, patting his shoulder in a reassuring way. "Calm down! You jumped a mile. I didn't mean to scare you."

Johnny sighed in relief. "It's you," he said, turning. "Dad, let's go."

"Go?" asked his father, blinking in surprise. "Right now? Don't you want to look around the carnival? You might find a ship model or—"

"I don't feel so great," said Johnny. That much was true. His stomach was lurching, and he felt as if he were about to throw up. "Too much sun or something," he mumbled.

"Okay," his father said, looking at him with some concern. "Come on. We'll hike over to the cabin."

They were staying at a little place called Pirate's Cove. It was like a motor court, with a dozen cabins arranged around a semicircular walk. The road that led to it was sandy and littered with shells. It was soft and crunchy underfoot and would not be a good road to drive on, but that was all right, because Live Oak Key was such a small island that no cars at all were on it. Everyone walked or rode bikes to get around.

After a ten-minute trek, Johnny and the major came to the tourist cabins. These stood on stilts six feet off the ground. They were made of weathered gray wood, with tin roofs that sounded like drums when it rained. Dusty green oak trees, their branches all gnarled from years of sea winds, shaded the tourist court. From the crooked limbs of the trees, long gray-green beards of Spanish moss hung down, swaying in every breeze. Though the cabins might have looked a hundred years old, they were modern enough to have air conditioners in the windows, and as soon as Johnny and his father had climbed up the front steps, unlocked the door, and walked in, Major Dixon turned their air conditioner on full blast. "You do look sort of green around the gills," he said to Johnny. "You're probably right. We overdid it out on the Gulf today. Tell you what, Johnny. You stretch out on the sofa, and I'll run over to the front office. They sell first-aid supplies there. Maybe they've got something for an upset stomach."

Johnny lay down, grateful for the cool blast of air rushing over him. He closed his eyes, but as soon as he did, he imagined that ghastly, grinning face again, and his eyelids flew open like window shades that had been tugged too hard. He gulped in deep lungfuls of air. The cabin was a little place, barely twenty feet wide by twenty-five feet long, but now it seemed cavernous to Johnny. He and his dad had stayed here before, and ordinarily he liked the compact little house, with its beds that had drawers underneath them for storing clothing, and its strange little triangular closets. Now, though, the place seemed haunted. Through the archway that led from the living room to the cluttered kitchen-dinette, Johnny could see the shadowy form of the refrigerator. It was the old-fashioned kind with a round compressor on the top. To Johnny it looked like a ghost looming in the shadows. He told himself to get a grip, but it was no use. He felt oppressed, as if something were weighing him down.

After a minute he heard footsteps coming up to the narrow porch, and then the door opened and Major Dixon stepped in. He was holding a small pink bottle of Pepto-Bismol. "This might help you," he said. "I'll get a spoon." He went through the archway and clicked on the kitchen light, and the ghost became just the noisy old refrigerator again.

Johnny heard his dad rummaging in a drawer. Silverware tinkled, and his father came back looking faintly puzzled. "Here you are," he said. He gave Johnny a spoonful of the sweet, faintly minty medicine.

Then Major Dixon went back to the kitchen. When he returned, he was carrying a slim, flat book. "I found this in the drawer under the spoons," he said. "Funny. I never noticed it before."

"What is it?" asked Johnny.

"A book that's handwritten in some kind of foreign language. Looks really old," replied Major Dixon. "I can't make head or tail out of it myself. I suppose someone who rented the cabin before us put it in the drawer and forgot about it. Well, finders keepers! You can take this as a souvenir. Maybe Professor Childermass will be interested in it. It looks ancient enough to be historical, anyway!"

Johnny took the book from his father. It was bound in

boards covered with marbled paper. Swoopy, swirly designs covered the binding, curlicues and splotches of yellow, red, and chocolate-brown. The spine and the corners of the covers were reinforced with dark brown leather that had aged to a crumbly grayish color. Johnny opened the book, releasing a sharp, dusty, spicy scent, the mysterious, delicious smell of old paper. It was the kind of aroma he usually loved. The shadowy shelves of the Duston Heights Public Library smelled just like that, and they had offered him many hours of excitement and adventure.

This time, though, the odor filled him with dread. It was, Johnny imagined, like the smell of a tomb full of dusty bones. Behind it he sensed centuries of weary time, years and years of hungry waiting. Waiting for what? Johnny could not say. He opened the book carefully. The pages inside were brittle and brownish yellow with age. The handwriting on them had faded to the color of pale rust.

But it was no handwriting that Johnny could read. The letters, if they really were letters, were bizarre loops and whorls and jagged lines, making the words seem slashed right into the paper. The writing crammed page after page, a tightly packed, crabbed penmanship. Here and there in the book were hand-drawn pictures of bizarre flowers with human faces, nearly shapeless things that might have been animals slouching along on their hind legs, maps without directions or scale. Even the cover felt wrong under his fingers, oily and quivering with a hateful sort of life. Johnny wanted to throw the book away from him.

But he remembered that Madam Lumiere had told him the dark birdlike shape was a protective spirit. That creature had told him to get in touch with "Professor Frizz-Face" as soon as possible, and now Major Dixon had suggested that Johnny take the book to Professor Childermass. "Professor Frizz-Face" had to be Johnny's neighbor, who wore a set of wildly sprouting white side-whiskers. That seemed too much like fate to Johnny. And there was something familiar about the voice too, something he could almost, but not quite, remember. He clenched his teeth and decided that the professor had to see this strange volume. He shut it and said, "Thanks, Dad."

That night, Johnny climbed into bed sure that he would not be able to sleep a wink. His room was tiny, with barely enough space for his narrow bed, a dresser, and a coatrack. The window looked out through trees to the Gulf of Mexico beyond. If Johnny sat up in bed and looked out, he could see the gleam of moonlight on water. Lots of times he had done just that, imagining that he was living in the 1700's, when pirate ships menaced these waters. Sometimes he could almost see them, black silhouettes leaning with the wind, their sails billowing as they sought ships to loot. Often he had dreamed about them.

Tonight, though, Johnny lay back in bed, his breath coming rapidly and shallowly. He mumbled all the prayers he could remember and thought of his friend Father Thomas Higgins in Duston Heights. He wished he had the priest's stern courage and faith right now.

Because the cabin had only one air conditioner, the major and Johnny always slept with their bedroom doors open. Before long, Johnny heard his father's snoring. It might have bothered anyone else, but Johnny found the sound comforting. He closed his eyes and tried to relax.

He had just drifted off to sleep when something awakened him. It was a sound. Not a loud sound or a sudden sound, but a soft, slithery one. Johnny sat straight up in bed. He was terrified of snakes, and he knew that in the South there were lots of poisonous serpents: copperheads and cottonmouths and the dreaded rattlers. Was one in his room?

He reached out a shaking hand to click on his bedside lamp. Then he froze, a horrible thought hitting him. What if a snake were draped over the lamp? What if it were waiting there in the dark, its mouth open and its fangs dripping?

Johnny began to shake with fear. He heard the sound again, and this time it was less like a hiss than like quiet laughter, as if someone or something were chuckling at him in a horrible whispery voice. He looked around frantically. The room was dark, but a rectangle of pale moonlight lay across his sheets. It spilled from the foot of the bed down onto the bare wooden floor. Johnny had dropped the strange flat book beside the bed when he had turned in. Now the moonlight touched the cover, not bright enough to show him any of the colors, but making the book look as if it were a dark opening into some other world.

Johnny stared at the book so long that his eyes watered. Minutes crawled by. The path of moonlight grew longer as the moon slid down the sky outside, heading for the Gulf and for moonset. The sound of his own pulse hammered in Johnny's ears.

Was the book *changing* in some way? Johnny squinted his aching eyes. Maybe it was a trick of the light, or of his watery vision, but the dark shape on the floor was wavering, dancing slowly, as if he were seeing it beneath clear but troubled water. From somewhere far away he heard a steady roaring sound. It was not like the gentle surf of the Gulf, a surge and a pause. It was more like the sound of a distant fire, hoarse and continuous.

What was happening? Part of him wanted to jump out of bed and run shouting to his father. But Johnny held on. He knew that his dad would think he had just had a nightmare. Somehow, Johnny hated to act scared or childish when his father was around. He knew the major was a very brave man. He had even been shot down behind enemy lines once and had single-handedly fought through to freedom. Johnny wished he could be like that. Now he was ashamed to run screaming like a little baby. He told himself he could take it, whatever "it" might be.

Then he saw it. A greenish shape rose slowly from the black rectangle on the floor, flowing out like vapor. It grew longer and longer, glowing with its own light. It began to curve across the floor, back and forth, as if it really were a snake. A snake made out of fog, not of flesh and blood.

Johnny thought he was going to faint again. He struggled to breathe. What if that terrible thing crept up the bedpost? What if he saw it slithering over his sheets, heading right for his face? What would it do to him?

He desperately wanted to look away, but he could not. He felt as if he were frozen. Now the serpentlike shape was ten feet long, writhing across the floor in loop after loop. It coiled, just like a rattlesnake getting ready to strike.

Johnny forgot about looking silly in front of his father. He opened his mouth to scream. Nothing came out but a mousy "e-ee-ee-ee" that no one outside the room could possibly hear.

The misty serpent reared, like a cobra ready to bite. The greenish head swayed back and forth. It was a head without a face, without features. Then it slowly turned. The creature flowed out the door in a long, sinuous stream. It vanished without a sound.

Still Johnny could not stir. He heard his father's snoring suddenly stop—

Johnny jumped out of bed, a scream just behind his teeth. He caught it before it escaped.

Johnny listened hard. The air conditioner hummed and sighed. The old refrigerator clattered and groaned. Crickets and cicadas zinged and chirred out in the Florida darkness. Johnny heard all these, but he did not lie down until he was sure he heard his dad's regular snoring again.

A dream, thought Johnny. I just had a dream. That's all. He reached out to turn on the lamp, hesitated, and then clicked it on. Yellowish light flooded the room. His wristwatch said it was nearly three in the morning. His shorts and shirt lay on the floor where he had tossed them, and beside them lay the book.

Johnny got out of bed. He reached for the book, but then changed his mind. Biting his lip, he grabbed his shirt and shorts and dropped them down on top of the volume. It was a childish action, he knew, like hiding under the covers to escape from an imaginary goblin.

Still, covering the book made him feel better. He turned his lamp off again, lay back, and soon was asleep.

This time he didn't dream at all.

CHAPTER THREE

Something really odd happened the next morning. Johnny and his father got up, showered, ate the last of their cereal and milk for breakfast, and packed. Not once did Johnny think about the strange book. Not even to notice that it had somehow, mysteriously, disappeared. When he picked up the dirty clothes he had used to cover the puzzling book, it was nowhere to be seen. But he forgot all about it in their rush to get their suitcases packed.

They took a little bright yellow speedboat to the sleepy Gulf town of Alachamokee, a scattering of filling stations, fishing supply shops, and general stores. In front of Art's Bait and Tackle, they caught a Greyhound bus to Tallahassee, where they boarded a train. Major Dixon had booked a sleeping compartment for them.

Johnny always enjoyed traveling on a train at night, lying in his berth and looking out the window at the dark countryside flashing past. He loved to imagine the stories taking place in the houses that he saw only as lighted windows. Sometimes they rattled through big cities too, splashes of neon lights roaring past like comets. Johnny didn't stay awake very long, though. The rumble of the train was somehow very soothing, easing him into sleep.

They arrived at Duston Heights the next day, early in the afternoon. Professor Childermass met them at the station in his maroon Pontiac. He was a short, elderly man with a wild nest of white hair, gold-rimmed eyeglasses, and a red, pitted nose that always reminded Johnny of a strawberry that had turned a little too ripe. As Johnny and the major stepped off the train, Professor Childermass took out his pocket watch, made a big show of looking at it, shaking his head, and then he snapped it shut. "About time!" he snarled. "Two minutes and thirteen seconds late! In my day the engineer would have to answer for that!"

Johnny couldn't help smiling. Professor Childermass had such a cranky temper that he terrified almost everyone in Duston Heights, and yet he and Johnny got along famously. The old man was, as he put it, out of uniform. He was wearing tan wash pants, a soft blue shirt, and bright red suspenders. "I don't have to dress up when I'm not teaching," he announced smugly. "I intend to spend the whole blessed summer being a slob!"

The professor bustled Johnny and the major into his car, and then took them on a quick, careening trip through Duston Heights and across the Merrimack River. Never a very good driver, the professor talked a mile a minute, turned halfway around in his seat. He complained of the hot, dry spell that had ruined his nasturtiums, and then he demanded to know how they had enjoyed their trip. Sometimes Johnny closed his eyes as they came roaring up to an intersection, but the professor somehow managed not to hit any pedestrians, signposts, or other cars. At last he turned onto Fillmore Street and drove up the long hill to Johnny's house.

Johnny saw Gramma and Grampa Dixon standing on the front steps. They smiled and waved as the professor brought the Pontiac to a halt with a screech of brakes and a pungent blue-gray cloud of smoke from the overheated tires. "Here they are, safe and sound, just as promised!" the professor bellowed as he flung open the driver's door. "Stuffed to the gills with tales of the fish that got away, no doubt! Come on, you two! We'll help you carry your bags inside, and then we want the whole story."

That was a happy homecoming. Johnny's grandmother was a short, white-haired woman who was a fanatical housekeeper. A speck of dust never had a chance in the Dixon house. She also happened to be a fabulous cook. In honor of the occasion, Gramma Dixon had made a delicious meal, a New England pot roast.

Professor Childermass, who taught history at Haggstrum College but whose hobby was baking, contributed a yummy, gooey Black Forest cake.

Johnny and the major distributed the souvenirs they had picked up in Florida: a hand-painted plate for Gramma, showing a marlin leaping from the water; a fancy leather spectacle case for Grampa with Seminole beads worked into it; and for the professor, a jaunty, long-billed red fishing cap, which he popped onto his head and wore for the rest of the afternoon. Gramma liked her plate, and Grampa seemed pleased too. Henry Dixon was a gaunt, tall, slightly stooped man with just a few strands of hair combed over his bald, freckled head. He also wore old-fashioned gold-rimmed spectacles, which he took off and slipped into the leather case. "Perfect fit!" he announced happily.

Later that afternoon Johnny's best friend came over. His real name was Byron Ferguson, but he hated to be called that and allowed only a few people, like the professor, to refer to him as "Byron." Most knew him as Fergie. He was a tall, skinny, dark-haired kid with a long, droopy face, jug ears, and big feet. Fergie was as good at sports as Johnny was at history and English, and the two of them got along really well. Fergie was kind of a smart aleck too, but Johnny could take his kidding and dish some of it right back at him. They had liked each other almost from the moment they had met at Boy Scout camp, and Johnny had picked out a dandy souvenir for his friend. It was a pocketknife with mother-of-pearl handles, but it had hidden talents. A little fork and spoon folded out of it, along with a saw blade, a file, and a regular knife blade. Fergie grinned as he thanked Johnny and shoved the knife down into his jeans pocket.

As twilight fell, Johnny and Fergie went for a long ramble down Fillmore Street. It was a clear New England evening, very cool after the muggy Florida weather. They strolled past old houses, going from one little yellow island of light to the next as they moved from lamppost to lamppost. Fergie had told Johnny that their friend, Sarah Channing, still wasn't home. Her dad taught English at the same college as Professor Childermass. He had taken Sarah and her mom on a long vacation to England. They wouldn't be back until the beginning of July.

"So, Dixon," said Fergie, "how was Florida this time?" The two walked by the weathered brick buildings that had once been shoe factories. Just ahead was the old iron bridge over the Merrimack River.

"Great," returned Johnny. "Dad and I went fishing on the Gulf just about every day."

"I noticed you were kinda red," said Fergie with a chuckle. "Just a little bit, sort of like a hard-boiled lobster. Wait'll that sunburn starts to peel. I'm gonna have to call you 'banana nose'!"

Johnny shrugged. "People with blond hair don't tan, I guess," he said. "On the other hand we are *lots* smarter than you poor souls with black hair!"

"Says you!" howled Fergie. He laughed, then asked, "Seriously, Dixon, did you get to hunt any pirate treasure? Did you learn about any crumbling, mysterious old parchment maps? Or at least bring home a new model ship?"

Johnny felt in his pocket. The coin the old woman, Madam Lumiere, had given him, lay cold and round there. He ran his thumb over the surface. The metal was so worn that it felt slick, almost greasy. He took it from his pocket and stopped beneath a streetlight. "I got this," he said, holding it out.

Fergie took it from him and examined it under the light. He gave a low, impressed whistle as it glinted in his grasp. "Cool! This is one of those old Spanish dollars. It's pirate loot, Dixon! This is what they meant when they said, 'Pieces of eight'!"

Johnny took it back from him. "You know why they called it that, don't you?"

Fergie shrugged. "I guess 'cause it was worth eight American dollars or something."

"Wrong!" Johnny told him. "It was because these coins could be split up into eight pieces. You could break it apart into eight little wedges, just like carving up a pie."

Fergie gave him an uncomprehending look. "Huh? Why would you want to do a crazy thing like that?"

"To make change," explained Johnny patiently. "If you bought something that cost a quarter of a dollar, you'd break off two of the pieces and hand them over. You know the football cheer, don't you? 'Two bits, four bits, six bits, a dollar'?"

"Sure," Fergie said. His eyes lit up. "Oh, I get it now! That's what each piece of the pieces of eight was, right? A bit! Touché, Dixon, you got me! If I was wearin' a hat, I'd tip it! Say, where did you get this beauty, anyways?" Fergie returned the coin to Johnny, who put it back into his jeans pocket.

Feeling vaguely uncomfortable, Johnny said, "I got it from a strange old woman. She told my fortune for a quarter, and she gave me this coin when she had finished."

Fergie snorted. "It can't be real, then. I mean, she'd hafta be out of her jug to swap you a real Spanish dollar for a measly quarter!"

"It wasn't exactly a swap," said Johnny slowly. Something was needling his brain. He felt as if he were right on the edge of learning something new, or of realizing that he knew more than he thought. But whatever it was buzzed away like an annoying mosquito as Fergie started to talk about the Red Sox, the school year they had just finished, and what they might do with the rest of the summer.

Finally he went home no wiser than he had been before they started the walk. That night, when he went to bed, he put the shiny Spanish dollar on his night table, right beside his glasses. He stared at it for a long time before he turned off the light. Somehow he slept a little better just knowing it was there.

Major Dixon left for his base in Colorado a few days later. He promised to be back home at Christmas, and Johnny said good-bye to him at the train station. For the rest of that day Johnny knocked around on his own. Fergie was busy helping his folks paint their bedrooms, and Johnny felt too lazy to volunteer to help.

He fooled around with his wooden model for a while, carefully painting the little fiddly bits: the ship's wheel, the cannon, the bell, and the lanterns. This time he was determined to do a shipshape job. He hoped to have a beautiful model schooner to show his dad when he came back in six months.

When Johnny got tired of that, he got a snack from the kitchen, Ritz crackers spread with pink pimento cheese, and a glass of chocolate milk. He took these out to the screened-in front porch, where he settled back in the swing and munched happily as he started to read. He had found *In Deadly Waters*, a dandy book on pirate lore, in the Duston Heights library.

Sipping his chocolate milk, Johnny read wide-eyed about the town of Port Royal, which had been wrecked by an earthquake in 1692. The book's author said that a whole section of the waterfront, a notorious pirates' den, had slipped right into the Caribbean Sea! Whole streets of taverns, inns, and stores lay there under thirty feet of water. Who knew what treasures were just waiting to be found?

That reminded Johnny of the Spanish dollar that Madam Lumiere had given him. He took it from his pocket and studied it. For some reason he had kept it pretty much a secret so far, showing it only to Fergie. Thoughtfully, Johnny nibbled the last of his crackers. He looked across the street at the big stucco mansion where Professor Childermass lived. Then he put a marker in his book, closed it, and hurried off the porch.

Banging on the professor's front door produced no answer, so Johnny went around back. There he found Professor Childermass on his knees, with a trowel in his hand. He wore his red fishing hat, and sweat poured down his face as he planted a whole crate of orange and yellow flowers. "There!" he snarled as he ripped out a wilted nasturtium and tossed it aside. "Die on me, will you! Faw! I'll put in a better flower in your place, you withered weed! To the rubbish heap with you, you vile vegetative vermin! Oh, hello, John."

"Hi, Professor," Johnny said. "Can I help?"

The professor settled back on his heels and nodded. "You most certainly can. The watering can is over there by the spigot. Fill it up and lug it over! I was hoping someone would come along and save my aching back!" He brandished his trowel. "Meanwhile," he growled, "I shall be rooting up these impertinent plants. By heaven, I'll force something to grow in these flower beds of mine, or I'll pave over the whole yard and paint the concrete green! See if I don't!"

Johnny brought the water over, and before long they stood up. The professor put his hands on his hips and nodded with a satisfied air. "Now, that's more like it," he said. "Nasturtiums are nasty! Anyone can grow a marigold, though. And I like them better, anyway!" He clapped Johnny on the shoulder. "How about a nice cool glass of lemonade?"

"Sure," said Johnny, smiling.

They went inside, and the professor went upstairs to the bathroom to scrub his hands and dash some cold water on his face. Then he came back down, took a frosty pitcher from the refrigerator, and poured two tall, icy glasses of lemonade. "You look as if you have something dark and desperate on your conscience, my fine feathered friend," said the professor as he handed Johnny his glass. "I suggest we retire to the study and then you can unburden yourself. Or if life has *really* got you down, you are welcome to use my fuss closet."

Johnny chuckled and shook his head. Professor Childermass was firmly persuaded that at times he simply had to let loose and roar and rant and rave about all the troubles in his life. He had fixed up the closet in his study for just that activity. He had lined the closet with athletic mats to soundproof it, and he had tacked a sign to the back wall: "To Fuss Is Human: To Rant Divine!" Whenever he got a traffic ticket or banged his thumb with a hammer while trying to do one of his many carpentry projects, he would go into the closet and scream, yell, and, well, fuss, for an hour or so. He claimed that the fuss closet kept his blood pressure down and gave him his unusually even disposition.

Johnny saw that, with college over for the summer, the

professor had tidied up the study. He had swept out the huge drifts of blue-covered exam booklets and term papers that normally cascaded off his desk. He had even put some of the books back into their places on the bookshelves. Others still lay piled on the desk and stacked on the floor. The professor pushed some of the books on the desk to one side, put his lemonade down, and settled back in his chair with his hands behind his head. "Now, John," he said, "what's on your mind besides your hair?"

"This," said Johnny, putting the coin on the desktop, where it lay gleaming in the light from the window. "Do you think it's real?"

The professor's eyebrows shot up. He picked up the coin and held it close to his face, squinting at it as he turned it around. "Interesting," he murmured. "Very interesting, indeed. Do you know what you have here?"

"A Spanish dollar," said Johnny promptly. "The kind that they talk about in the pirate stories when they write about pieces of eight."

"Bingo," replied Professor Childermass. "Also bull's- eye, home run, and A-plus. If I recall, this is a type of coin called a 'cob.' I can barely make out two numbers here. I think they're a five and a six, which means this little beauty was probably stamped in 1756 or 1656. I think I have a book on old coins somewhere that might tell us more. Let me find it."

Professor Childermass went to a tall bookcase beside the door. He stood on tiptoe, muttering to himself as he read the titles on the spines of the books. While he did that, Johnny sipped his lemonade and looked at the professor's stuffed owl, a wise-looking bird whose wisdom seemed slightly under par because of the miniature Red Sox baseball cap it wore at a rakish angle.

And as Johnny looked at the bird, something went click! in his head. He suddenly saw, in his mind's eye, at least, the dark shape of the bird hovering above Live Oak Key Lighthouse. And he heard again the voice that had warned him in Madam Lumiere's tent.

"Aha!" roared the professor, dragging a tall book from

the top shelf in a billowing cloud of dust. He sneezed hard and then said, "I knew that I—"

"Professor!" shouted Johnny at the same moment. He leaped to his feet and gave Professor Childermass a wild glance. "Brewster! Whatever happened to Brewster the Rooster?"

Johnny had yelled louder than he intended. His shout must have startled the professor, because he dropped the heavy book right on his foot. The old man squinched his eyes and whistled. He didn't yelp in pain, though. Instead, he turned slowly. "That," he said, "is a very curious question. Very curious, indeed. John, why on earth did you choose this exact moment to think of Brewster?"

Johnny now knew why the bird and the voice had seemed so familiar. They belonged to a being, a spirit who claimed to be Horns, an ancient god of Upper and Lower Egypt. Some years before, the professor had discovered a wonderful time-traveling trolley in his cellar. He had brought a black bird statuette back from the temple of Abu Simbel in ancient Egypt, and the figure turned out to house the spirit of Brewster. The professor had called him that because the statue reminded him of "Brewster the Rooster," the trademark of Goebel's Beer. After the professor had gotten rid of the Time Trolley, Brewster had also gone away.

Until now, anyway.

Johnny blurted out his story. "I'm almost sure it was him," he finished. "Brewster, I mean, trying to warn me."

The professor picked up the book about ancient coins and went to sit in his chair. He took a long drink of lemonade. "Strange, very strange," he murmured. "Also uncanny and unsettling. You see, John, I've been having weird dreams for the last couple of days. And guess who has been the featured player in them all?"

"Brewster?" asked Johnny.

"Brewster," replied the professor in a grave, troubled voice.

CHAPTER FOUR

Johnny asked, "Whatever happened to Brewster, Professor? He was with us when we went back in time to Constantinople, but after we got back, he disappeared."

Professor Childermass crossed his arms and leaned back in his chair. The light from the window behind him made his white hair glow almost like a halo in a picture of a saint. A crabby, red-faced saint. He cleared his throat and said, "Well, John, you remember Aurelian Townsend, the inventor of the Time Trolley, and how he took his blasted contraption back into the past. As for me, I had had my fill of time traveling. You may not know, though, that Mr. Townsend visits me from time to time. On his first visit I asked him to take Brewster's statuette back to Egypt, around the year 3000 B.C., and drop it off in a nice little temple. I knew Brewster would enjoy being worshiped as a god far more than he would be willing to endure being gawked at as an exhibit in a museum."

"But now Brewster's come back to the present," said Johnny. "How did he manage that without the Time Trolley?"

Professor Childermass tapped his chin with his finger. "I don't think he really *has* returned, John. Brewster is a spirit, and spirits don't live in time quite the same way you or I do. Evidently he is trying to communicate with us. That is why you're seeing visions of him and why I'm having peculiar dreams. Yes, Brewster wants to attract our attention, but I gather that, without the onyx statuette, he is having great difficulty in getting through. The falcon statue gave him his focus and let him speak to us."

Johnny thought for a moment. "Maybe the statuette still exists in the ruins of that temple in Egypt."

With a snort the professor said, "Oh, certainly. By now, no doubt, the statuette is cozily buried under fifty or a hundred feet of Egyptian sand. And a fat chance we'd have of finding it too! Hmm. Too bad Aurelian Townsend took the Time Trolley with him when he moved permanently to the 1890's." He drummed his fingers on the desk and hummed an unmusical tune. "Maybe I can do something about Brewster's problem and help him get in touch with us," he said at last. "I have a friend in New York, and you can find practically anything in New York."

"What are you trying to find?" asked Johnny.

With a smug look Professor Childermass said, "Never you mind. If I can pull it off, it will be a surprise for you. I'll call my friend later today. However, first we have the problem of this rare Spanish coin to look into." He opened the book and began to leaf through the pages.

Johnny came around to stand beside him. The book had columns of black-and-white pictures of coins, showing both the front, or obverse, side and the back, or reverse, side of each one. Paragraphs described each set of photographs. The professor found a section on Spanish coins from the New World and went through the pictures of the gold and silver pieces very carefully. "That one looks a lot like it," Johnny pointed out.

"Right you are, John," the professor said, bending close to the page. He put his stubby forefinger on the text below the picture. "Let's see.... The types of coins called cobs were cut from a one-ounce bar of silver or gold. The word 'cob,' by the way, is a shortened form of a Spanish word meaning 'cut.' Well, an ounce of silver was cut up into eight pieces. Then the pieces were heated, flattened out, and roughly shaped into a circle. Very roughly in some cases. In fact, yours looks decidedly more like a coin than most of these do. The designs were then hammered into the metal with steel dies. Hmm. This coin of yours probably dates from 1656, because the design on it wasn't used in 1556, and by 1756 they were minting regular milled coins. So your souvenir is three hundred years old! Real history right in your pocket, John!"

Johnny felt very solemn at the thought of owning something that had existed before the United States had even been a nation. "It's more than just a coin, though, Professor. It was supposed to be pirate booty, and Madam Lumiere said it was a good-luck charm," he said.

The professor shrugged. "It has a cross on it, of course, and that is a symbol of good. And I suppose that if enough people have believed this little blob of silver was lucky over the years, some of their belief may have soaked into it. I'm not exactly a superstitious man, John, but if you think this trinket will bring you good luck, I really and truly hope it will." He read another passage in the coin book. "Anyway, it seems likely that this coin was made somewhere in Spanish America in the year 1656. My guess is that it was minted in Potosi, or in modern terms Bolivia, because that's where the ones with better workmanship originated. And it may very well have been part of a pirate's treasure. In the sixteenth and seventeenth centuries, Spanish galleons sailed from the Caribbean to Spain loaded to the scuppers with gold and silver, and pirates loved to prey on them."

Johnny picked up the coin and held it on his palm. He let the light from the window catch it as he tilted the coin to stare down at the faint impression of the cross stamped into the ancient silver. The figure was like a capital *T*, except that the crossbar went right through the center of the vertical line. The ends of the crosspieces were flattened out, so the design looked like this:

Just staring at the cross gave Johnny a mysterious, peaceful feeling, and he felt his mind clearing. Then he started. "Oh, my gosh!" he cried, his eyes wide. "I forgot about the book! I forgot all about it!"

"This book?" asked the professor, holding up the one he was reading. Behind his spectacles, his eyes were wide and questioning.

"No, the one that my dad found down on Live Oak Key in Florida," replied Johnny. He shook his head. "How could I have forgotten it? It scared me half out of my mind!" His words tumbling over each other so that Professor Childermass had to slow him down a couple of times, Johnny explained about the book and the weird feeling it had given him. He told about the nightmare too, and the strange, snaky, misty thing that had seemed to rise from the tome as it lay on the floor. Professor Childermass listened, a frown of concentration making deep lines on his face.

When Johnny finished, the professor pulled at his nose. He looked intensely troubled. At last he grunted and said, "Mysteriouser and mysteriouser, as old Lewis Carroll might have put it." He leaned across the desk, his eyes glittering behind his gold-rimmed spectacles. "Tell me again about the writing you saw in this book. Was it Arabic? Chinese? Egyptian hieroglyphics? Would you recognize the language if I could show you a sample of it?"

"I don't think so," replied Johnny slowly. "It's hard to explain. I mean, the marks looked like letters, but they didn't look like a real language, if you understand me."

"Not exactly," answered the professor. He growled in his throat, as he sometimes did when feeling frustrated. "It sounds like a real puzzler. Very well! I'm going to call my old friend Charley Coote and ask him if he knows anything about that sort of book. He's an expert in magic, after all, and this tantalizing tome you're describing sounds as if it might be magical. What did you do with the wretched thing, by the way?"

Johnny wrinkled his forehead in thought. "Nothing," he said slowly. "That's the strangest part of the whole story. I don't know what happened to the book. It just disappeared from where I dropped it."

"Your father didn't pick it up?" asked the professor. "Think, John. It might be important."

Johnny shook his head. "No. It was in my room, and he didn't even come in there the next morning. I'm pretty sure Dad forgot all about the book too. Anyway, he never mentioned it to me again after that night."

Professor Childermass sighed. He raised his hands in mock surrender. "Babbling birds, sinister snakes, and vanishing volumes! Well, this is too deep for me! What did the poet Robert Burns say? 'The best laid schemes o' mice and men gang aft a-gley.' Know what that means?"

Johnny, sure that the professor would tell him, shook his head.

"It means," said Professor Childermass, "that no matter how well you plan and plot, fate always comes along and heaves a monkey wrench into the works! Take me, for example. I thought I was going to take the summer off and loaf, bake cakes, and beat you at chess. Libraries and books and research projects were the last things on my mind, but your adventure down in Florida calls for a little investigation. Tell you what, John. Give me a couple of days to work on these problems. We'll drop the whole subject until then, unless you manage to recall anything more about this blasted book that gave you the galloping woo-hoos. After I've found out a thing or two, we'll get together and see what's what. Is that agreeable?"

"Sure," replied Johnny, and they left it at that.

During the next two days, Johnny fretted only a little over the mysterious book and the lucky coin. Most of the time, he and Fergie found plenty to do, and when Johnny was busy, he didn't have time for worrying about possible disasters.

He and Fergie rode their bikes all over Duston Heights. They went looking for arrowheads in the park past Emerson Street, where a brook meandered among a chain of ponds. Sometimes in dry weather they found the arrowheads sticking out of the soil among the stones in the banks of the brook. Fergie had quite a collection of them, with the best ones displayed on black velvet in a wood and glass frame.

When they got tired of amateur archaeology, the two boys gobbled rich, gooey banana splits or hot fudge sundaes in Peter's Sweet Shop, an ice-cream parlor with an old-fashioned soda fountain. Johnny liked the marble counter and high stools and deep wooden booths with curly sides. There were colored glass lamps, and a jukebox, plus a display case up in front with boxes of candy in it. The soda shop always smelled friendly, its air sweet with chocolate and vanilla and spicy with cinnamon.

After they had stuffed their faces, Johnny and Fergie went to an afternoon matinee at the movie theater and sat through a double feature of horror films, *The Beast from 20,000 Fathoms* and *It Came from Beneath the Sea*. One movie was about a giant octopus terrorizing San Francisco, and the other about a dinosaur that had been frozen in the Arctic ice but came to life. Johnny and Fergie found both films more funny than scary, and Fergie laughed so hard during the second one that a grumpy usher shone his flashlight at the two boys and threatened to throw them both out.

They spent some time in the cool, dusty stacks of the library, reading up on Spanish treasure and pirates. When they felt cramped from being inside, they played long games of flies and grounders. Fergie was much better at baseball and all other sports than Johnny would ever be, but Johnny had come along with some coaching from Sarah, and now he didn't feel quite so helpless with a bat or a ball in his hands.

In other words, Johnny and Fergie enjoyed the gorgeous summer. The season was still young. June was not even halfway over, and exciting weeks stretched out ahead of them before school would start again in the fall. The two friends knew how much fun they could cram into those weeks, and both of them looked forward eagerly to the rest of the summer.

On Saturday afternoon Johnny and Fergie rode their

bikes back from the park after a long session of flies and grounders. As they whizzed through Duston Heights, Johnny was in the lead, with Fergie behind him, weaving his bike back and forth and pretending to be the pilot of a fighter plane. "You're in my sights, Dixon!" he yelled now and then. "Better take evasive action! I'm firin' my fifty-caliber machine guns! Ack-ack-ack-ack-ack! Zzz-aaa-oww!" People they passed looked at them as if they were both crazy.

They pumped up the long hill on Fillmore Street, past the vacant Barton house two doors down from the professor's house. They turned sharply to the right and rolled into Johnny's yard and let their bikes fall clattering to the grass. Gramma Dixon was in the front parlor, reading a magazine and listening to dance music on the radio. She greeted Johnny and Fergie with a smile as they headed for the kitchen, where Johnny poured chocolate milk for both of them. "Johnny," Gramma called, "remember, Grampa wants you to mow the lawn this afternoon."

"Okay," Johnny yelled back. He asked Fergie, "Want to help?"

Fergie rolled his eyes. "Sure, John baby! I *love* to spend my Saturday afternoons slavin' away instead of havin' fun!" He lifted his chocolate milk. "Here's to the workers of the world! All they have to lose is their lawn mowers!"

Johnny shrugged. "Well, you don't have to if you don't want to. I can do it myself."

"Nah," said Fergie with a grin. He wore a mustache made of chocolate milk, but Johnny didn't point that out. "It's faster an' easier if we take turns. And the sooner we get work outa the way, the sooner we can dream up somethin' fun to do. I hate to admit it, John baby, but I'm already startin' to get a little bored with the summer."

So they dragged the lawn mower out and started on the backyard. Despite Gramma's frequent suggestions, Grampa Dixon had refused to buy a gasoline mower. The only sort he liked was the old-fashioned push kind, with big black rubber wheels and shiny spiral blades that made a metallic whirring noise when you rolled it along. Grampa Dixon insisted that the push mower did a neater job, and it was cheaper too, because it ran by muscle power alone.

The lawn mower required a lot of that. Leaning forward as he mowed, Johnny pushed it, fascinated by the green arc of grass clippings that it sent spraying up. Grampa was right about one thing. The mower did leave the lawn smooth and level as a billiard table. Johnny did half the backyard, then Fergie took over and finished the job. After drinking a glass of water apiece, they dragged the mower to the front of the house and began working on the lawn there. Grampa, who had been upstairs taking a nap, heard them and came out with his clippers and tidied up the hedges.

Johnny sighed as he started on the last strip of long grass. If he could have had any wish in the world just at that moment, it might have been for summer to go on forever just like this, with him having fun with Fergie (and, when she got back, with Sarah), his family happy, and no cloud of worry on the horizon. Even work didn't seem much of a hardship when he shared it with Fergie, and the whirr of the lawn mower, the snip-snip-snip of Grampa's clippers, seemed like just another kind of music, like the summer songs of cardinals and crickets.

It was a wish that would not come true. Johnny didn't know what terrible events were about to burst upon him.

CHAPTER FIVE

For some time Professor Childermass did not have any news for Johnny. Then, right after lunch on Monday, Johnny recognized an old blue Chevrolet parked at the curb in front of the professor's house. It belonged to Dr. Charles Coote, a specialist in the folklore of magic who taught at the University of New Hampshire. Johnny hurried across Fillmore Street to see what news Dr. Coote had brought.

Professor Childermass met Johnny at the door. He held the screen open with a broad smile of welcome on his face. "Greetings, John! I was just about to call you over when I glanced through the screen door and saw you coming. Charley just got here, and he has some information that may pertain to the book you found down in Florida. No, don't ask questions. He hasn't told me a solitary thing yet. Come on up to the study, and we'll see what he knows."

Dr. Coote was waiting for them. He sat in the overstuffed armchair near Professor Childermass' desk. A tall, weedy, slightly stooped man with fluffy white hair, a long, ridged, bent nose supporting horn-rimmed glasses, and the air of an absent-minded professor, Dr. Coote smiled at Johnny. "Hello," he said, opening a thick manila folder on his skinny knees. "Well, this time you gave me a poser! However, I may have learned a thing or two that might help, so sit down and I'll tell you about invented languages and mysterious books."

Johnny took the straight chair on the other end of the desk, with the stuffed owl at his right elbow, and Professor Childermass settled himself in his rolling chair behind the desk. "All right, Charley," he said. "We're all ears."

Dr. Coote coughed. He made a tent of his fingers and

peered over the top rims of his spectacles. "Ah, first, perhaps Johnny should describe this book to me as precisely as he can. I only know what Roderick has told me, you see, Johnny, and he's rather elderly and forgetful."

"Elderly! Forgetful!" erupted Professor Childermass. "Why, you pompous pedant, I—I challenge you to a brain-wrestling match!"

"Never mind him," said Dr. Coote with a wink at Johnny. "Just tell me the story in your own words, as they say in the courtroom dramas."

"And whose words do you *think* he'd use?" asked Professor Childermass with a snort. "Robert Cawdrey's? Samuel Johnson's? Noah Webster's? They all wrote dictionaries, didn't they?"

"Please, Roderick," scolded Dr. Coote with mock severity. "Go ahead, Johnny."

Closing his eyes to imagine the strange writing and drawings, Johnny described the odd book as well as he could. Dr. Coote listened with a look of concentration on his thin features, nodding encouragingly now and then and sometimes tapping the tips of his fingers together thoughtfully. When Johnny finished, the elderly man shuffled through a thick stack of papers in his folder. "Let me see, let me see," he murmured. "Hmm. Yes. Was it anything like this?" He handed Johnny a slick sheet of photostat paper.

Johnny took it from him. The photocopy showed a page of strange cursive writing, with a peculiar plant rising through the words. The plant's roots spread out along the bottom edge of the page, its stem rose and curved to the left, and from it hung flowers that looked like church bells. Johnny had studied Latin in school, and the letters looked a little like the old-fashioned Latin manuscript letters used by monks in the Middle Ages. The markings were not real letters, though, and they made no sense. "It was sort of like this," said Johnny. "The letters were different, though. Some of these look like *a*'s and *o*'s, but the letters in the book that I saw didn't resemble any alphabet I know of. Where did this come from, Dr. Coote?"

"From the Voynich Manuscript," answered Dr. Coote. "The original is hand colored and is actually rather attractive, in a bizarre sort of way. This black-and-white copy really doesn't do it justice."

Professor Childermass pounded his fist on the desk. "Charley! You're a scholar, not some kind of art critic! What in thunder *is* this manuscript? You never tell a story the right way! Begin at the beginning!"

Dr. Coote smiled and coughed again. "Well, Roderick, that is a bit difficult to do. You see, no one really knows where the true beginning, well, begins. In this century, the manuscript was discovered by a man named Wilfrid Voynich. He found it at the Jesuit college of the Villa Mondragone in Frascati, Italy, and purchased it in the year 1912. He published a description of it in 1921, and not long after that he made photostatic copies available to scholars. No one who has seen the manuscript has ever been able to read it or even to make a guess about who wrote it, or when. Some people believe it may date all the way back to the English scholar and magician Roger Bacon, who lived in the late 1200's. Clues in the manuscript suggest that it is in some kind of code, but no one can even determine the language in which it is written, much less decode the message. It has been a deep, dark mystery ever since Mr. Voynich discovered the work."

"And where does that leave us?" asked Professor Childermass.

Dr. Coote shrugged. "Nowhere, I'm afraid. There are other peculiar books from the medieval period with strange symbols in them, but most of these have to do with alchemy and magic. What Johnny describes sounds much more like the Voynich Manuscript than anything else—that is, an herbal."

"Terrific," snarled the professor. "We have no clues at all."

"What is a—an herbal?" asked Johnny.

Dr. Coote answered him: "An herbal is simply a description of plants. The Voynich Manuscript includes some pictures of anatomy too, along with other things, but a large part of it is taken up with drawings of various flowers and other kinds of flora. Except the plants pictured are not of this world."

"Oh, wonderful," growled the professor, his face getting redder by the second. "What world are they from, then? Martian melons? Plutonian plums? Moon mushrooms?"

"Now, now, Roderick." Dr. Coote shifted uneasily in his chair. His mild face took on an expression of vague worry. "The truth is, no one knows what strange realm of time or space may be pictured in the Voynich Manuscript. Perhaps it is totally imaginary. Or just possibly, it is a place that one could not reach by automobile, ship, or airplane. It may be another, ah, region altogether."

"Peachy," muttered Professor Childermass. "Just peachy. Well, if we can't get there by streetcar, I'm not planning to go! Now, have you anything to suggest, Charley? Anything practical, that is?"

"Only the obvious." Dr. Coote gave Johnny a sympathetic smile. "It would help if I could actually examine this book. Unfortunately, I gather the chances of that are slim."

Johnny felt as if he were letting his friends down. He hung his head. "I don't know where it is," he said in a small voice.

"Well, I think—" began the professor, only to be cut off by a sharp ring from the telephone downstairs. "Drat! Let me see who that is, and it had better not be a wrong number!"

While he was gone, Dr. Coote said, "One thing might help. You say the manuscript you found was bound like a book. Describe the binding for me."

Johnny did his best. When he had finished, the old man said, "The binding was probably done late in the last century. The kind of marbled paper you describe was frequently used in bookbinding from about 1880 on. From your description, though, the pages inside the binding sound as if they are much older. Perhaps even medieval. Were they regular paper?"

"I think so," said Johnny slowly. "They didn't look like parchment."

"Possibly vellum," reflected Dr. Coote.

Professor Childermass came back into the study, a smile

of satisfaction on his face. "John," he said, "that was the post office. They are holding a package for me. My friend in New York sent it C.O.D. for some reason. Would you be willing to ride your bicycle into town and pick it up for me?"

"Sure, Professor," Johnny said, rising from his chair.

Professor Childermass took his wallet out and pulled a five-dollar bill from it. "This will more than cover the postage, and you may keep the rest for your trouble. Bring that package back, and we'll see if there is another way of understanding exactly what happened to you in Florida."

It wasn't a long ride to the post office. Johnny stood in line at the barred window and asked for the professor's package. After paying the C.O.D. charges, he pocketed the change and lifted the package from the counter. It was a rectangular box perhaps a foot long by six inches wide and six inches deep. It had been wrapped in brown paper and tied with green cord, and it was fairly heavy, a couple of pounds at least. A red-bordered address label had the professor's name and address on it, with the return address listed as "P. Shellmacher, 1291 Stuyvesant Circle, New York."

Wondering what could be inside the package, Johnny climbed aboard his bike and zoomed across town to Fillmore Street. He found Professor Childermass and Dr. Coote still in the study, Dr. Coote sitting with his knees drawn up so his thin legs looked like an elderly, angular cricket's, and the professor pacing impatiently back and forth. "Aha!" exclaimed Professor Childermass as Johnny entered with the package. "Now let's see if this helps."

With an air of deliberate mystification, Professor Childermass took the box from Johnny, placed it on the desk, and used his penknife to cut the cords. He tore the brown paper away, revealing a cardboard box, its lid Scotch-taped shut: Grunting in irritation, the professor sliced through the tape and opened the box. He took out something wrapped in layer after layer of white tissue.

"For heaven's sake, Roderick," said Dr. Coote. "Is this like one of those Russian dolls, with another doll inside it, and another inside that one? Does the wrapping go on forever?"

"No, Charley," returned Professor Childermass tartly. "It ends right here!" He ripped away the tissue paper, revealing a shiny black statuette of a falcon.

Dr. Coote's shaggy eyebrows climbed toward his hairline. "What in the world is that supposed to be?" he demanded. "The Maltese Falcon?"

"This happens to be a statue of Horus, a god of Upper and Lower Egypt," responded the professor haughtily.

Leaning close to the figure, Dr. Coote peered at it for a moment. Then he straightened and said querulously, "It isn't authentic."

Professor Childermass blushed. "Well, no. This is only a replica, made of Bakelite. A company in New Jersey turned 'em out by the carload back in the twenties, when there was a big fad of Egyptian art and decorations. My friend in New York City scoured the antique stores before she found this."

Dr. Coote blinked at the professor. "I don't see what it— wait a minute. *She?* Roderick, you old rascal, who is this woman of mystery?"

"None of your beeswax," said Professor Childermass. "She is an old and trusted friend, and that is all you need to know."

Johnny was itching to know why the professor had ordered the statuette. He asked, "Professor, is this about Brewster?"

Professor Childermass caught himself, smiled, and said, "Indeed it is, John. As you see, this is about a half- size reproduction of the Horus statuette I found in Egypt—"

"When were you in Egypt?" asked Dr. Coote suspiciously.

"For two hours in the late afternoon of March fifteenth, 14 B.C.," retorted the professor. "The weather, in case you are wondering, was dry. We went to Egypt in the Time Trolley, which you know about. I'll tell you the story one day. However, now I want to try a little experiment."

With a smug, confident expression, the professor picked up the nine-inch-tall figurine. He held it by the base and lifted it to his mouth as if it were a microphone. Slowly and distinctly, he said, "Roderick Childermass calling Horus! Roderick Childermass to Horus! Come in, Horus! Over!"

Dr. Coote's jaw dropped almost all the way down to his chest. He stared at the professor, then at Johnny. He asked, "Is Roderick playing some practical joke, or should we wrestle him to the floor and call for a straitjacket?"

"Charley, please!" said the professor. "I have to concentrate!" To the statuette, he said, "Horus! Brewster! If you have something to say to us, confound your feathery hide, do it now! This is Roderick Random Childermass calling Horus, also known as Brewster the Rooster! If you're there, talk to me!"

"Really, Roderick, what you're holding is *not* a sacred relic, but just a cheap—" began Dr. Coote.

He never finished. With a sudden, enormous crack! a bolt of lightning sizzled just outside the study window, turning everything to a dazzling white. Spots danced in front of Johnny's eyes. An instant later, thunder shook the whole house, and then rain began to pour in torrents.

Johnny had yelped in alarm at the lightning bolt. His ears rang from the thunder. Dr. Coote leaped from his chair, his eyes wild. "The day was perfectly clear!" he shouted. "Where did this storm come from?"

Professor Childermass grimaced. "Not so loud, Charley!" He turned and glared out the window at a world that had suddenly turned gray with rain. "I hope my calling Horus didn't have anything to do with—"

"Look!" said Johnny with a gasp. He pointed his shaking finger at the windowsill.

Streaky red liquid crawled over it. It looked horribly like blood.

"A rain of blood!" roared Dr. Coote. "Like one of the plagues of Egypt!"

Johnny's teeth chattered. The strange rain somehow was creating a picture. It was much sharper and clearer than a TV picture, and it seemed three-dimensional. A craggy-faced man smiled at him, seeming almost real. "That's Dad!" Johnny exclaimed.

Then a terrible thing happened. The major's eyes grew wide and frightened. He opened his mouth and screamed, though Johnny heard no sound. And his face tore apart. His body burst open, like a cocoon splitting. From inside it emerged a creature whose flesh was dark green, like an insect's. It had huge faceted eyes and a human mouth set in a look of hateful triumph. It pushed the body of the major away, and it stood swaying like a gigantic praying mantis, its pincer claws ending in humanlike fingers with sharp, long nails clenching and unclenching.

Suddenly, hard rain drummed on the window, normal rain. The terrifying vision blurred, melted, and ran. In an instant it had dissolved.

"What in the name of heaven?" whispered the professor. "The rain is stopping. It's over!"

Johnny swallowed. The rain had ended with unnatural swiftness, as if someone had turned off a gigantic shower in the sky.

Again the telephone downstairs rang, and again the professor hurried to answer it, leaving Johnny and Dr. Coote in the study. Dr. Coote mopped his face with a handkerchief. Then he reached out a shaking hand, picked up the falcon figurine, and studied it. He looked on the bottom of the base, adjusted his spectacles, and read, "Made in Grover's Mill, New Jersey." He sniffed and set the statuette down. "You wouldn't think a little thing like this would—"

He broke off as the professor's voice came from downstairs, its pitch and volume rising at the same time. "Now, Henry!" he bellowed. "Be calm. You have to be calm! Let's all be VERY CALM!"

Johnny said, "He's talking to Grampa!" He jumped out of his chair and hurried downstairs, with Dr. Coote clattering close behind him. He saw Professor Childermass hang up the phone and then slump against the hallway wall. "Professor!" Johnny said, alarmed. "What did Grampa want? What's wrong?"

The professor turned slowly, his face pale. In a low voice, he said, "John, I am very sorry. It's bad news."

"What?" Johnny asked, feeling cold all over. "What is it?"

The professor took a deep breath. Reluctantly, he said, "I'm afraid—well, John, I—" he gulped, squared his shoulders, and finished, "I'm afraid it's about your father."

CHAPTER SIX

"Gravely ill."

The haunting words kept repeating themselves over and over in Johnny's brain as the airliner descended above a mountainous landscape. When the airplane's tires hit the runway with a bump-bump bump! the rhythm seemed to echo "gravely ill." It was like a tune he couldn't get out of his mind. A frightening, threatening tune.

For those two words were the message that Gramma and Grampa Dixon had received from the Air Force. Major Harrison Dixon was gravely ill. It was hard for Johnny to believe that the long-distance telephone call had happened only a day ago. Professor Childermass had taken charge at once, arranging for airline tickets for himself and Johnny. He pointed out that there was nothing that Kate and Henry Dixon could do, that the trip might be an exhausting one, and that he would try his best to arrange for Major Dixon to come home. They agreed at last, after the professor promised to stay in touch by phone every day.

The professor haggled with an auto-rental clerk, then he and Johnny climbed into a new-smelling Ford for the long drive. Johnny had never seen the Rocky Mountains before, but he was so worried that the high, snow-covered peaks meant nothing to him. The professor hunched over the steering wheel, occasionally swearing under his breath at a hairpin curve or another motorist. "John," he said at last, "maybe you had better get out the map and help me navigate. I've stapled the directions to the hospital to the map. Look sharp! We don't want to miss this forsaken little town!"

Johnny unfolded the road map of Colorado that Professor

Childermass had bought before they left Massachusetts. They were driving to a small town named Talus, where Major Dixon was in the hospital. The Air Force doctors didn't know how to treat him, so they had moved him to a civilian hospital. "Just as well," the professor had said when he first heard that news. "The base where your father works is a top-secret site, so we probably couldn't have visited him there."

Leaning over the map, tracing their route with his finger, Johnny said, "We're still about fifteen miles away. We'll cross a river, and then we have to turn left."

Grimly clutching the wheel, the professor nodded. "Very well. Are you hungry, John? If you are, we can stop and grab a bite in town. I'm sure these westerners at least know how to fry a hamburger!"

Johnny sighed. The fear he had felt when he saw the terrible vision of his father in the rain of blood still lingered. "No, thanks, Professor. I don't really feel like eating right now."

"I understand," said Professor Childermass gently. For a few minutes he drove without speaking. Then he whistled and said, "Whoops! When you said we'd cross a bridge, you weren't kidding! Look up ahead."

Johnny lifted his gaze from the map. The bridge was a long, green metal suspension structure. It was no different from many other bridges Johnny had seen. But it spanned an enormously deep chasm.

The Ford rumbled onto the bridge, and Johnny looked out the side window. He and the professor were in bright sunlight, but the gorge beneath them lay in deep, purplish shadow. Far down—so far that it looked at least a mile away—a pale silvery-blue river snaked in great loops among red and orange rocks. Johnny swallowed hard. Flying didn't really bother him. At least, flying in an *airplane* didn't. However, the thought of the professor at the wheel and the view of how far the drop would be if the car careened off the bridge combined to make Johnny's stomach feel a little fluttery.

But they got across without any problem, and before long

they rolled into Talus, which Johnny thought looked like a town in a western movie. A broad, dusty main street ran between blocks of wood, stone, and brick buildings. Many of them had high false fronts, and some had arches like the ones Johnny had seen in pictures of the Alamo. Lots of the men on the sidewalks wore jeans, boots, and cowboy hats. Johnny noticed them, but he was feeling more and more nervous and worried, so he paid little attention to his surroundings. "The hospital should be right ahead," he told the professor. "According to these directions, it's supposed to be on the main street."

"And there it is, just to our right," related Professor Childermass. He slowed in front of a three-story brick building with a big black-and-white sign reading "St. Catherine's Hospital" on its lawn. He parked the car, and after he got out, he put a gentle hand on Johnny's shoulder. "Now, don't worry. I'm sure your father's condition probably sounded worse than it actually is. Doctors love to make people's flesh creep!"

But when they got to see Major Dixon, his condition was very, very bad. He lay unconscious, with an IV bottle dripping a yellowish fluid into a needle stuck into his arm. Johnny thought his father looked withered and gray, with dark circles under the major's closed eyes. His breathing was alarmingly slow.

The doctor, a heavyset, gray-haired man with thick glasses and a soft voice, said, "We simply don't understand what has happened to him. His vital signs are not that bad. And the major is in good physical shape. We know that he hasn't had a heart attack or a stroke, and X rays don't show any tumor or other problem. He simply did not wake up yesterday morning, and the Air Force doctors were as baffled as we are."

Johnny held his dad's hand. It lay limp in his grasp. Tears stung Johnny's eyes. He had lost his mother years before, and now he was terrified that he might lose his father too. He felt hopelessly fearful of what the future might bring.

The professor asked, "Could Major Dixon be moved to Massachusetts? That's where his family is."

"I don't see why not," said the doctor. "We can't really do anything for him here, and possibly specialists from Boston might think of something we haven't. Of course, moving him could be very expensive, but perhaps the Air Force would help out. I'd have to insist that he be flown there. I wouldn't want an unconscious patient making a long trip by ambulance. And in order to move him, you would have to have the Air Force's permission."

"Don't worry about all that," said the professor decisively. "I can take care of the expense, if necessary. As for the Air Force, well, I'm an old military man myself. I'm sure I can persuade the powers that be to allow Major Dixon to recuperate at home."

The doctor smiled. "I am sure you can, sir," he said. "You strike me as a very forceful personality."

The professor solemnly shook hands with the doctor. "You are a rare specimen indeed, Doctor," he said. "A physician who recognizes that not all intelligent people have 'M.D.' tacked on after their names!"

During the two days that Johnny and the professor stayed in Colorado, the major's condition did not improve. Professor Childermass persuaded the Air Force to fly Major Dixon to Boston, where an ambulance would transfer him to the Duston Heights hospital. Other than that, nothing happened to ease Johnny's worries or his deep sense of gloom.

The professor and Johnny were staying at a hotel in Talus. It had small rooms with tiny, cramped bathrooms. Professor Childermass stayed in room 221, and Johnny was right across the hall in 222. The beds were comfortable enough, but the rooms certainly were not fancy. The hotel did have a few good points, though. All the windows looked out on incredible mountain views, with bare peaks marching off into the distance. The clear air made them all sharp and vivid, purple, gray, and black rock and glistening white snowcaps. If Johnny had felt better, he would have enjoyed the experience.

The hotel also had a restaurant and gift shop. As they sat down to breakfast in the restaurant on their last morning in Colorado, the professor looked at Johnny over the rims of his spectacles and said, "Well, John Michael, neither of us has mentioned it. But we have both been thinking it, so we might as well drag everything into the open. Your father isn't really ill, not as the doctors understand illness. He must be under some sort of horrible curse."

Johnny nodded. "That's what I think," he confessed. "And, Professor, it's even worse. It's my fault."

The professor blinked in surprise. "What? How can you possibly believe that? "

Johnny began to sob. He wasn't exactly crying, but his chest heaved and made it hard for him to get his words out. "B-because I-I w-went into the t-tent and Madam Lumiere r-raised that ghost! That's where it all s-started!"

"Easy, easy," said Professor Childermass in a comforting tone. "Why, John, you didn't cause anything. Sometimes events just happen. But rest assured, my friend, we will not leave your father in the lurch. The first thing to do is to get him safely home, so that Henry and Kate don't worry themselves sick over not being able to see him. And just as soon as we do that, you and I—and Byron too, because we may need his brains and muscles—will return to Florida and find this mystical medium. If anyone can help us to understand how all this ties in with the ghostly figure you saw and the strange book you found, she's the one." The professor stopped speaking as a waiter came to take their orders.

When the waiter had left them, Johnny said, "I don't know if she can help us. She seemed kind of thrown when her crystal ball went haywire."

"She can give us knowledge," pronounced the professor decisively. "And knowledge is power."

As soon as the two of them had been served, he dug into his breakfast, a big western omelet oozing with tomatoes, peppers, cheese, and onions. "Never say die, John!" he declared as he munched. "We have been in dire straits before this, and we've come through with flying colors! Now, eat your buckwheat pancakes, or I may reach over to your side of the table and devour them. This mountain air gives me the appetite of a starving cougar!"

Johnny nodded and poured syrup over his pancakes, though he still didn't feel very hungry. The two of them ate silently until they finished their breakfast. The professor paid, and they started over to the elevator, planning to go to their rooms and pick up their bags. Johnny paused in front of the gift shop. He pointed at something in the window. It was a tiny bird, carved from some kind of black wood and hanging as a pendant on a rawhide thong. "Could I buy that?" he asked.

"What on earth for?" asked the professor. "It's only a tourist trinket. Probably made in Japan!"

Johnny took the silver coin from his pocket. "I was thinking that I could put this on the cord and hang it around Dad's neck," he explained. He gave the professor a weak smile. "It's supposed to be good luck, after all."

The professor nodded. "Very well, John," he said. "But if it costs more than fifty cents, I think it would be smarter just to find a leather shop and buy a plain old shoelace. They cost only a dime!"

They bought the small carving. The bird it represented, the professor said, was probably a thunderbird. "That was an imaginary creature that was so huge, its wings blotted out the sky," he declared. "The thunderbird is part of the mythology belonging to many of the original native peoples of the West, from the Great Plains to the Pacific Northwest. This is a pretty handsome piece of carving for a gimcrack touristy bangle. After you take it off the rawhide, hang on to it."

As it turned out, though, Johnny didn't take the carved thunderbird off the thong. He couldn't figure out any way of hanging the silver coin without putting a hole through it, and he didn't want to do that. So in the end, he decided that he would wait until they were back in Duston Heights to solve the problem. He would hold on to the peso de ocho reales until then, and he would hang the thunderbird pendant around his own neck in the meantime.

They returned to the hospital, where Johnny sat in the waiting room while Professor Childermass worked out the details of moving Major Dixon. The room was sunny and warm, and Johnny nodded off to sleep. Before long, he began to dream.

It seemed that he got up and went to his father's room. A doctor was bending over the major's bed. The man wore the white uniform of a hospital doctor, and he appeared to be checking Major Dixon's heartbeat. "Is Dad going to be all right?" asked Johnny.

The doctor slowly straightened up, his back to Johnny. He was tall. Impossibly tall. His head brushed the ceiling. Slowly, the figure turned. Johnny felt paralyzed. He could not run or even scream.

The doctor wore a surgical cap and a mask that showed only a slit of his features. He reached up and whisked the mask away. Johnny saw a horrible face, the face of the spectral serpent. It flowed and changed and became the bug-eyed image that he had seen in the rain of blood! The monstrous mouth gaped at him, its sharklike teeth clashing, and reddish spittle drooled out. Then the face changed again and became a human skull leering at him. A hoarse voice burst from the skull: "He will be mine! I will devour his soul and become strong! And then the world will die!"

Johnny screamed as everything went black. He opened his eyes again and found he was still sitting in the waiting room. It had all been a nightmare. Or had it? Somehow, a sick feeling grew in the pit of Johnny's stomach. Maybe it had not been just a dream. Perhaps he had glimpsed some terrifying apparition that had evil plans for his father and for him!

He ran to Professor Childermass, who listened calmly to his story. The old man patted his shoulder. "It's only a dream, John," he said. "I have them myself when I'm under stress. Don't worry. We'll do all we can for your father, just as soon as I show these hospital people who is the boss!"

Everything was arranged at last. An Air Force ambulance took Major Dixon to the base so that he could be flown to Massachusetts. Johnny and the professor drove back to Denver, where they returned the rental car and boarded an airliner for the long flight back. By the time the plane took off, night was beginning to fall. The professor sat in a bright pool of light from the overhead panel. His white hair gleamed, and the light glistened on the rims of his glasses as he sat reading a magazine. Once they were airborne, Johnny peered out the oval window. He could see the airplane's wings with their huge engines, blinking lights, and whirling propellers. As the plane rose higher and higher, it climbed from twilight into sunlight. All around them the sky was a pure, clear blue. It reminded Johnny of that last day in Florida, when he had felt so happy aboard the fishing boat. He silently said a prayer for his father, remembering the Psalm that begins:

Deus noster refugium et virtus adiutor in tribulationibus quae invenerunt nos nimis.

The Latin words meant, "Our God is our refuge and strength: a helper in troubles, which have found us exceedingly." Johnny felt that his troubles had found him more than exceedingly. In fact, he felt surrounded by them.

And then Johnny heard someone say, "Pssst!"

Johnny looked around. "What?" he asked.

Professor Childermass glanced up from his magazine, his eyebrows rising. "I beg your pardon, John?"

"I thought you said something," Johnny told him.

"Not me," answered the professor.

"Psst!" It was louder this time.

Professor Childermass looked flummoxed. "I heard it that time," he said. "If it wasn't you, I hope the airplane hasn't developed a slow leak!"

Johnny looked around. He and the professor were in

almost the last seats in the airplane. An elderly lady across the aisle was asleep. The two seats in front of them were empty. "Who said that?" asked Johnny in a whisper, beginning to feel alarmed.

"I did!" The voice was faint and sounded as if it were coming from far away.

"Brewster!" said the professor. His voice was so loud that the lady across the aisle woke up and gave him a sharp look. He turned away from her, as if he were talking to Johnny, and then went on more softly, "I'd know that voice anywhere! Confound you, you feathery fiend, why didn't you speak to me when I tried to get in touch with you?"

"Keep your hair on, Whiskers!" the voice snapped. "There are good reasons for everything. Look, I can't say much or do anything right now. I'll help you two all I can, but just talking to you is very hard for me. Johnny, don't throw away the carved bird you bought! It's letting me break through to you. And don't despair! There's hope!"

"That's good news," growled the professor. "Tell us about it!"

"Later," said the voice, becoming fainter. "Communicating with you now is difficult. Later, I promise. But I have to warn you—you are both in terrible, terrible danger!"

And then the voice was gone completely. Johnny and Professor Childermass stared at each other. Neither of them spoke.

There was nothing to say.

CHAPTER SEVEN

A few days later Johnny, Fergie, and the professor stepped off an airplane into the humid heat of a Florida afternoon. Johnny blinked in the bright sun. Although the month was only late June, the day was hotter than the hottest August day he could ever remember. "Whoo-oo-oosh!" said Fergie, taking off his Red Sox baseball cap and fanning himself with it. His curly black hair stuck to his skull in gleaming rings. "Talk about an oven! No wonder you were so red when you got back from Florida, John baby. You can get charcoal-broiled just by walkin' around outside!"

"We are not here to discuss the weather, Byron. Come along with me, gentlemen," said Professor Childermass brusquely, pushing open a glass door and bustling into the airport building. "The car-rental agency is supposed to have a nice sedan all ready for us. I, for one, want to get to the island before nightfall!"

"Yeah, sure," said Fergie, lugging his suitcase through the door. "Maybe we can find this Madam Whoozis in a hurry and then get back to a cooler climate. Man, I can't believe how hot it is! This is like living in a steam bath!"

Johnny didn't say much. He was still far too worried about his dad and his grandparents. Major Dixon had been successfully moved to the Duston Heights hospital, where Professor Childermass had given strict orders that the Dixons' family physician, Doctor Carl Schermerhorn— whom he considered a quack—was not to treat the patient. A younger, very serious specialist named Nesheim took the case instead, although he was just as puzzled as the doctors in Colorado had been.

Johnny had last seen his father the previous afternoon, when Gramma and Grampa Dixon had stood helplessly beside their son's bed. Gramma was crying and holding on to the major's limp hand, while Grampa stood quietly with tears rolling down his loose, leathery cheeks. Major Dixon lay as still as death and did not seem to know they were there.

After leaving the hospital, Johnny had spent a half hour at St. Michael's Church, lighting a candle for his dad and kneeling to say prayers for him. He had hoped to talk to Father Higgins, but the priest was away at a conference.

Adding to Johnny's worries was the fact that, despite Brewster's promise, the spirit had not spoken to him again. Johnny wore the thunderbird amulet around his neck all day, and at night he kept it close beside his bed. Still, he had not heard another peep from Brewster. Johnny felt as if he were spending his life on pins and needles. Brewster had warned them, but what was it that he warned them about? When a kid had the kind of imagination Johnny did, he could dream up all sorts of dire disasters. Not knowing what the warning was supposed to be about was far more frightening than anything Brewster could have told him. Johnny lost his appetite and a lot of sleep, and sometimes he feared that he was losing his mind.

At the car-rental desk the clerk handed the professor the keys, and he led the boys outside to a year-old black Pontiac, an automobile the professor said he understood very well.

They stowed their suitcases in the trunk. Then, in a cloud of exhaust smoke, they set off, driving south on a two-lane asphalt highway lined with palm trees. It was so hot that mirages formed on the road ahead of the car, wavery sky-blue patches that shimmered and danced and looked just like shallow pools of water. They magically evaporated as the car sped toward them, without leaving a trace behind. Johnny and Fergie shared the backseat, with both of their windows rolled down so a blast of air washed over them. It was so muggy that Johnny felt as if he had just climbed out of a hot swimming pool, but the breeze did help a little.

They drove for a long time, and finally they saw a sign that read "Alachamokee 15." An arrow pointed to the right, and the professor steered the Pontiac onto a narrow, rough road that needed repaying. As they jounced and bounced, Johnny, who was sitting on the right, nudged Fergie and pointed through the window. Fergie leaned over to look. The Gulf of Mexico could be seen through gaps in the roadside palm trees. From the glimpses they got, the water looked as flat and shiny as a sheet of scuffed aluminum. Fergie started to hum, and then he burst into song. "By the sea, by the sea, by the bee-yoo-tiful sea," howled Fergie in an ear-splitting tone, missing the tune by a mile.

"Ouch!" said the professor, wincing with his whole body. He turned around and glared over his shoulder. "Mister Byron Q. Ferguson, if you don't want to walk the last twelve miles, kindly pipe down!"

"Aye, aye, Captain," answered Fergie with a broad smirk. He clapped his friend on the shoulder. "C'mon, John baby," he said. "We'll fix up your old man. All we have to do is find the witchy woman, right? She'll know what to do."

"I hope so," said Johnny, although what he felt was more despair than hope.

They rolled into the sleepy town of Alachamokee just after four o'clock. The professor drove up and down the narrow main street until he found Gator Gus's Boating and Fishing, a little sun-baked cinderblock building with a badly faded sign above its door. It had been painted white at one time—Fergie suggested that had been shortly before the Civil War—but now the hot sun and the salt air had blistered and peeled most of the paint off, so the gray concrete blocks showed through, splattered with splotches of green mossy lichen.

"Here's where we're supposed to leave the car," grunted the professor, edging the Pontiac into a cramped alley. "And then the ferry is supposed to be a short walk away. Judging by the accuracy of the information I've gotten so far, I suppose that means it's not quite as long a walk as it would be to Omaha, Nebraska!"

Behind the store was a parking lot with three slots marked "Rentals Park Here." All of these were empty, and the professor pulled into the middle one. The three of them climbed out into the sweltering afternoon and got their suitcases from the trunk. Looking around, Johnny got his bearings and said, "The water taxi is this way."

He led them about a block west, where the alley dead-ended into a highway. On the far side of this road was the Gulf of Mexico—or at least the Alachamokee Bay part of it. Dozens of sailboats and powerboats were tied up at piers along the shore. There wasn't any traffic on the highway, so the three sauntered across and found the booth where they bought tickets for the ride over to Live Oak Key. As they walked down the pier to the bright yellow speedboat, Johnny pointed out the tall white spire of the lighthouse. "I saw Brewster right there," he said. "I thought he was a real bird."

"He's a real pain in the behumpus," griped the professor. "If I'd known he'd shilly and shally the way he's been doing, I would have told Mr. Townsend to drop him down a nice, deep well in Egypt."

"Aw, Prof, I kind of liked old Brewster," teased Fergie. "Even if he was a worse singer than me."

"Fergie," Johnny said, "*no one* is a worse singer than you."

The professor looked surprised, but then he barked a short laugh. "Congratulations, John," he said. "That is the first faint trace of a joke I've heard from you in ages. Keep your spirits up! Now, let's climb into this disreputable craft and pray that it doesn't sink before we reach the distant shore."

They roared across the mile of water separating the mainland from Live Oak Key. "Man, this is better!" announced Fergie, holding on to his baseball cap as the cool bay breezes whipped his shirt. "I could go for this kinda life. If I lived in Florida, I'd have a boat just like this an' I'd stay on the water for twenty-four hours a day!"

Once they reached the island, the professor spied a ramshackle wooden shop called The Sand Dollar Store. A tattered poster beside the door announced that bicycles could be rented, and soon the two boys found themselves on twin red Schwinns with big, fat balloon tires that wouldn't sink into sand. They rode with their suitcases across the handlebars. Behind them the professor pumped along on a slightly rusted blue bicycle. He had lashed his suitcase to the rear fender, and he was quite a sight as he sat upright on the seat with great dignity, his chubby legs moving like pistons to push the pedals.

They rode down the dirt road toward the Pirate's Cove cabins. "Look at me, John baby," crowed Fergie, leaning back. "No hands!" He raised his hands off the handlebars and rolled along with a smug smile on his face. Johnny was always too afraid of falling to try that trick. It was not so much that he feared getting a bump on the head. He was far more scared of getting a bad scrape and coming down with a deadly tetanus infection. Johnny was terrified of tetanus, or lockjaw. He held on tight to his handlebars.

"One side, amateur!" roared the professor. Fergie grabbed his handlebars and swerved over to the right, ahead of Johnny. He looked around in bug-eyed astonishment as the professor pedaled serenely past, his arms folded across his chest. He stuck out his tongue at Fergie and winked mischievously. "I was doing the no-hands trick before your father was born!" he announced. "Watch me and learn a thing or three!"

Just by leaning this way and that, the professor made his bike swoop gracefully from side to side. Fergie laughed his head off. "Better get a grip, Prof," he yelled. "If anybody sees you, they'll think a performing bear escaped from the circus or something!"

"Says you!" returned the professor, but he did put his hands back on his handlebars. "John, unless I'm mistaken, that is our destination just ahead. I've reserved the same cabin that you and your dad stayed in. I hope that won't bother you."

"No," said Johnny truthfully. In fact, he felt comforted by

being back on Live Oak Key, where he and his father had enjoyed their vacation so much.

They went into the main cabin, the one with the little newsstand and store and the check-in desk. A skinny, sour-faced, middle-aged man was behind the counter. He wore a loud Hawaiian shirt with pink and purple parrots all over it. The man was even shorter than the professor, and he had a head of spiky, rusty-red hair that bristled in all directions like a worn-out broom, except for a shiny pink bald spot right on the top of his head. As the professor asked for the key to the cabin, the man said in an irritable, whiny voice, "You din't say there was gonna be three o' you. That's an extry five dollars a night!"

Johnny braced himself for an explosion, and indeed the professor began to puff himself up like the frog in the fairy tale, the one that tried to pump himself up to the size of an ox and finally blew himself to pieces. But the professor ground his teeth so loud that Johnny could hear the grating noise. Finally the old man simply grunted. "Very well," he snapped, and he pulled out his wallet and counted the money, slamming every bill on the counter. "And I shall certainly be sure to tell all my many Florida-bound friends of your hospitality!"

Fergie said he had never seen a house raised up on stilts before, and he clambered up the steps, unlocked the door, and plunged right in. Before Johnny had even crossed the porch, he heard the air conditioner clatter to life.

The professor took the bedroom that Major Dixon had used, and Johnny got his old room back. Fergie happily announced that *he* planned to sleep on the sofa, right in front of that magnificent air conditioner. As soon as they had unpacked their bags, they changed into more comfortable clothing. The professor had brought his red fishing cap along, and he perched it right on top of his head. He wore baggy tan walking shorts, a bright blue T-shirt, knee-high white socks, and tennis shoes.

Fergie stuck with his jeans, but he did change to a plain white short-sleeved shirt. Johnny wore his shorts and a cool, jacket-like denim shirt his dad had bought him on their previous trip. Beneath it, the thunderbird charm hung around his neck on the leather thong. It felt odd against his chest, as if the carving were somehow warmer than it should be. And it made his skin feel tingly, not quite itchy and not quite sunburned.

"Well, gentlemen," said the professor as he looked at his gold pocket watch. "It's time to decide on our next tactical move. Now, I for one am starving. Before I waste away to a mere shell of myself, shall we first find a place to dine and then begin snooping around to find some trace of this Lumiere person? Or—"

"Hey, Whiskers!" called a voice from thin air. "You can stuff your face later! The first thing you have to do is get the grimoire! In case you don't know what that is, it's a book of magic spells. Be careful, because this one is very ancient and extremely evil! Johnny knows what I'm talking about. Well, glom on to that little booby prize! And do it pronto!"

Fergie laughed out loud, and Johnny felt relief well up inside him, as welcome as cool water in the middle of a burning hot desert. There was no mistaking that quarrelsome, raspy voice.

Brewster was back.

CHAPTER EIGHT

Johnny pulled the thunderbird amulet out of his shirt. It swung on its leather thong as if it were alive. "Take off this rope!" ordered Brewster's irritable voice. "Then I might be able to help!"

The rawhide strip ran through a clip behind the thunderbird's head. Johnny untied the knot and pulled it through and, as soon as it was off the thong, the little carved wooden bird rose into the air and hovered above them. The professor said, "All right, you poor excuse for an antediluvian deity, where is this blasted book?"

"How should I know, Whiskers?" shot back Brewster. "This is *your* world, not mine! By the way, how am I coming through?"

"Loud an' clear," said Fergie. "Say, how come you weren't able to talk to us before?"

"Dark forces are working against me!" said Brewster, making his voice sound mysterious. "Forces on my side as well as on the earthly side! Besides, it helps if there is a focus of power on the earth. If Fuzz-Face here hadn't sent my statuette back to ancient Egypt, it would be no sweat. As it is, I have to make do with this foreign carving!"

Professor Childermass snorted. "Look, you frustrating fowl, I *tried* to get in touch with you through a replica of your figurine. Why didn't you cooperate then, eh?"

The little carved thunderbird jittered in the air. In an agitated voice, Brewster said, "That was a fake, and you know it! It wasn't a real temple figure at all, just an—an unreasonable facsimile thereof! For the trick to work, somebody who believes in me had to create the figure! And the gumps who worked in that factory in Grover's Mill didn't believe in much of anything beyond a weekly pay envelope!"

"Hang on, Feathers. Whoever carved this thunderbird pendant didn't believe in you either," said Fergie sarcastically. "They were Cheyenne or Sioux or something, not Egyptians. They never heard of Horus!"

The thunderbird image spun to face him. "It was me, anyway!" Brewster declared. "I was the thunderbird, just as I was Horus! After all," he added, sounding temperamental, "when the Egyptians stopped believing in me, I still had to work, didn't I? So I got a job as the thunderbird to tide me over!"

"Please," said Johnny, "let's not waste any more time. We have to find that book! Brewster, is it around here? Can you give us a clue?"

"A clue?" asked Brewster. "You mean like saying, 'You're getting warmer'? Sorry. I'm on *this* side and you're on *that* side, and just as you can't see the spirit world, I really can't see your world. All I can tell you is that unless someone has moved it, the cursed thing is still in that house. Be careful! It's more like a live creature than a book, and it has soaked up a lot of evil. It may be tricky! Now go scatter and find it! And let me know when you have! Whoosh! I have to rest now!" The floating bird figure dropped to the floor as if someone had cut an invisible string. Johnny picked it up and tucked it into his shirt pocket.

"You heard him," the professor said sternly. "Scatter! I'll take my bedroom. Byron, you search this room. John, look in your bedroom. Then we'll all tackle the kitchen, and if we don't find anything, we'll trade off rooms and look again! Go!"

Johnny hurried to his bedroom. It had not changed much since the last time he had been in the cabin. The spread on the bed was now dark blue instead of dark green, but that was about it. He dragged a chair over to the closet door and stood on it to peek on the little triangular shelf above the clothes bar. Nothing but dust. He looked in all the drawers beneath the bed. Empty. Then he had a sudden inspiration and pulled the drawers themselves all the way out. But the book wasn't beneath the bed either, or under the mattress or jammed between the head of the bed and the wall. Nor was it propped up against the windowsill behind the curtains. And there just wasn't any other place to look.

Johnny went back to the parlor and found that Fergie had cheerfully taken everything apart. The sofa cushions lay scattered over the floor. The radio, a big old wooden table model shaped like a Gothic arch, had been taken off its stand beside the sofa. The coffee table had been turned upside down. Fergie had even rolled up the throw rugs. "Any luck?" Fergie asked.

Johnny shook his head. "It isn't in there," he said. "I guess you didn't find anything either, huh?"

"Oh, yes I did!" retorted Fergie. "I found thirty-seven cents in loose change! Plus a Hershey bar that some kid dropped between the sofa cushions about thirty years ago! But no book."

Professor Childermass came out of the other bedroom, his hair bristling, and shook his head. "The kitchen," he said. They all went in there, and they poked everywhere. Johnny remembered that his dad had first found the book in a drawer, so they pulled out and emptied every drawer. They looked in the oven and in the refrigerator. They opened the cabinet beneath the sink and surprised a mouse. But they did not find the book.

They did succeed in making an incredible clutter. The professor sat down on the kitchen floor amid a pile of knives, forks, pots, pans, and dishes. "If Brewster hadn't all but sworn that fool book was here, I'd give up," he grumbled. "I don't see how it could be hidden anywhere we haven't looked, because we've looked everywhere."

"The bathroom!" yelled Fergie.

The professor shook his head. "I've searched the bathroom."

"Maybe," Johnny said slowly, "it's *under* the house. After all, we're up on pilings."

So the three of them trooped out and went under the

house. The gray earth beneath was bare, with little funnel-shaped dimples in it where ant lions, predatory bugs that looked like a Martian's nightmare, had dug traps for ants. Overhead were the joists and supports that held up the floor of the cabin, but there was no book.

"Well," began the professor, "I for one—"

"I can help."

The three had thought themselves all alone. At the sound of the voice, Johnny jumped like someone who'd received an electric shock. The professor started too, and gasped, "Holy H. Smoke!" as he spun around. Even Fergie's usually sleepy eyes popped wide open.

A woman stood nearby. "I saw you when you passed my house," she said.

"Madam Lumiere!" shouted Johnny, seeing the figure of the old woman beside the front steps of the house. He, Fergie, and the professor crept out, and Johnny introduced her to the others. Quickly he told her about the book and about his father's illness.

"No," she said solemnly. "He is not sick. He has been taken."

"Aw, no, lady," said Fergie. "He's in the hospital an' everything. The only place he got taken to was a private room in Duston Heights."

"His spirit has been taken," replied the old woman firmly. "And if you cannot find some way to return it soon, the body will die."

Madam Lumiere went inside the cabin with them. She stood in the living room, looking all around her as she turned in a slow circle. The professor cleared his throat. "Ahem. You will have to pardon the mess, my good woman. We have been rather busy."

Madam Lumiere nodded, her face empty of expression. "I sense a strong force of magic here," she said. She glanced at Johnny. "Johnny, do you still have the lucky token I gave you?"

"Yes," said Johnny, taking the peso de ocho reales from his pocket.

From somewhere among the folds of her dress, Madam

Lumiere produced a crystal ball, smaller than the one Johnny had seen in her tent, hardly larger than a baseball. It gleamed in the light from the windows. She held it out on her open palm, and Johnny could see reflections of the room weirdly distorted and upside down. "Hold the silver piece flat on your hand," directed Madam Lumiere. "Be sure the side with the cross is upward."

Johnny was beginning to have a creepy feeling, as if something was about to happen that might be dangerous. But he held the coin out, making his hand as steady as he could.

Closing her eyes, Madam Lumiere began to chant softly. Johnny, Fergie, and the professor leaned close to listen, but whatever language she was speaking was unknown to them. Johnny felt the silver piece on his palm grow warm. He looked at it in surprise as a ray of brilliant white light shot out from the center of the cross to the crystal ball, which glowed with its own light. Then the ray flashed back out of the crystal and straight up to the ceiling.

They all tilted their heads back as they looked up. The spot of white light on the ceiling began to make bigger and bigger circles, like ripples that spread out when you toss a pebble into a pond. Finally, when it had covered the whole ceiling, the round patch of light stopped just above the door to Johnny's bedroom. "In there," said Madam Lumiere with a groan. "Johnny, put the coin in my free hand." She held out her trembling palm, and Johnny carefully placed the silver piece in it. "Good. Now, you go! I must not move."

Johnny, Fergie, and the professor dashed into the bedroom. The late afternoon sunshine streamed in through the window. The spot of light reappeared on the ceiling although Johnny was sure that no ordinary light—like the beam of a flashlight, for instance—could have reached from where the sorceress was standing to there.

The spot of light slowed. It drifted to a dark corner of the ceiling, near the foot of Johnny's bed. Johnny narrowed his eyes, trying hard to see. The ceiling was made of plywood painted a flat white and supported by a couple of crisscrossing beams of dark wood. Was there something odd about that corner? He could make out a sort of irregularity—

The professor snapped on the ceiling light. "Look at that, by Gadfrey!" he said. "Just like a chameleon!"

Johnny felt the hairs on his neck prickling. The open book was there, with one cover pressed against the ceiling, the other against the pine-paneled wall. The part against the ceiling was the same flat white color, and the part against the panel was the same yellow as pine. It even had the streaks and whorls of wood grain in it, and one dark brown pine knot.

"No wonder we couldn't find it," said Fergie. "It's hard for me to see it now, an' I know just where to look."

The professor ran into the kitchen and came back carrying a straight chair. "I'll have it down in a jiffy," he proclaimed, placing the chair in the corner. He climbed up on it, but grunted in frustration. He was about two inches too short to reach the book. He jumped down and said, "Fergie, you have the build of a basketball player. Get up here and use those long arms of yours."

Fergie hopped onto the chair and reached up. He would have no trouble, Johnny saw. But then—

Yelping, Fergie jerked his hand back! The book had flopped over, flattening itself against the ceiling. For an instant they saw the brown, aged pages and the weird writing, but then the open book became a horrible gaping mouth, ringed with sharp, sharklike teeth! It made a vicious snap, missing Fergie's fingers by less than an inch!

Fergie ducked down as the book opened again. Drool leaked out of the mouth, and it made a nasty coughing roar, like the sound a tiger makes before killing.

"Leave this place, I command you!" The sharp sound of Madam Lumiere's voice made Johnny's head snap around. She stood swaying in the doorway. In her left hand, she held up the Spanish coin, pinched between finger and thumb so the cross showed. She pointed toward the book with her right hand. She had her pinkie and her index finger extended, and her middle and ring fingers folded down against her palm. "Depart this realm, evil spell!" she said, her voice as sharp as the crack of a whip.

For a moment the air around the terrible mouth seemed to *bend*, making everything ripple and shimmer. Then, with a growl, the book snapped shut and dropped to the chair, where it lay closed. Its covers were just the way they had looked the first time Johnny had seen the book: marbled paper and leather reinforcements at the spine and corners.

"Is it safe t' pick up now?" asked Fergie. "I don't want my friends t' hafta start callin' me 'Four-Fingers Ferguson.'"

"The spell has been lifted," said Madam Lumiere, slumping against the doorjamb. "It is as safe as such magical creations ever are."

"Allow me," said the professor, picking the book up gingerly. He opened it and scowled down at the pages. "Hmm. Just as John described. Bizarre, weird-looking flowers. Shapes that look as if they might be letters from an unknown alphabet. Well, now that we have possession of this booby prize, the next step seems to be learning what to do with it! Madam, have you any suggestions?"

"I must rest," mumbled Madam Lumiere. They helped her into the parlor, where she sank gratefully into the armchair. She gave the coin back to Johnny and sighed. "I am no longer so young as once I was," she said. "The struggle between the light and the dark takes much out of me."

"Thank you," said Professor Childermass sincerely. "Without your help, we would have accomplished nothing."

For the first time since Johnny had met her, Madam Lumiere smiled weakly. "One does what one can," she said. She took a few deep breaths. "Johnny, you are fighting an evil spirit. Three hundred years ago, he walked the earth as a man. Have you ever heard of Captain Damon Boudron?"

Fergie had collapsed onto the sofa. He bounded to his feet. "Bloody Boudron, the Scourge of the Spanish Main!" he said. He turned triumphantly to Johnny. "The pirate, remember? We read about him! Even his pirate buddies were scared of him. They said he fought with the devil standin' at his right shoulder! He was more interested in killin' his victims than in takin' gold from them!"

"I remember," Johnny said. "They called him Demon Boudron."

"Yes," agreed Madam Lumiere. "And the fact is, he was not human at all. He was in truth some spirit from the dark regions, disguised as a man. Who knows what his wicked purpose was? It was said that no man could kill him. He died on the seventh of June, 1692, but not by ordinary means."

"The earthquake," said Johnny. "That was the day of the great Port Royal earthquake in Jamaica."

"Yes," said Madam Lumiere. "And that was when the pirate Boudron was swept into the depths of the sea. But his evil did not end. Ever since then, his restless spirit has been trying to break through again—"

"Excuse me," came the sound of Brewster's voice. "This is all very interesting, but you people might want to know that someone who means you no good is creeping up on this house right now. If I were you, I'd run for it!"

CHAPTER NINE

Madam Lumiere rose and said, "I can help you no more. Be strong! And follow the lead of your spirit guide." She hurried out into the growing twilight.

The thunderbird carving flew up in front of Johnny's face and hung in the air, practically vibrating. "Shake a leg! Get a move on!" Brewster ordered. "If Nyarlat-Hotep gets wind of what you've done, all Hades will break loose!"

"Nyarlat Whosis?" asked Fergie. "Just what are you talkin' about?"

The little bird spun and jittered in an agitated way. "Nyarlat-Hotep! That's what Damon Boudron's name is in the spirit world! And he's *not* a nice creature from beyond the bounds of space and time. So don't just stand there with your face hanging out! Go!"

The carving swooped back into Johnny's shirt pocket, and the professor snapped, "Pack your kits, gentlemen! We're breaking camp!"

He took the book into his bedroom while Johnny ran to his room and tossed his clothes willy-nilly back into his cardboard suitcase. He could hear Fergie doing the same. Within minutes, Johnny, Fergie, and the professor were bustling out of the house. They started down the steps when a nasty voice said, "What's th' matter? Ain't my place nice enough for ya?"

From the gathering darkness of evening, a man stepped forward. He was the owner of the motor court, the thin little fellow with the bald patch surrounded by bristly red hair. "Where ya off to?" he demanded.

"We have business elsewhere," said the professor, stepping

ahead of Johnny to confront the man. "Of course you can keep the money I paid you, but we have to leave at once. Something came up very unexpectedly."

The man spat onto the sandy ground. "Yeah. I just *bet* it did. When I caught sight o' that ol' witch leavin' the place, I said to myself, 'Andy McDuff, you jist better make sure them three ain't stealin' you blind.' So I come over t' take a gander. You know what, fellas? I think you boys had jist better open them suitcases."

"Nonsense!" roared the professor so loudly that the riot of night insects fell silent for a moment. "You don't happen to have a little thing called a search warrant, do you? It just so happens, my ungrammatical friend, that the United States Constitution protects people against unreasonable searches! Now stuff that in your pipe and smoke it!"

The little man grimaced unpleasantly. He stood in a yellow square of light that came from a front window of the cabin. Johnny saw that McDuff had very bad teeth, what was left of them, McDuff took a stride forward, putting one foot on the bottom step, just below the professor. He said, "Yeah? Constitution, huh? Well, it *also* just so happens that I'm an official sheriff's deputy. I'm the law here on Live Oak Key, mister. An' if I goes in there an' see you've messed up th' place, why, I can toss you in th' clink for vandalism an' malicious mischief. Then I'll get t' look through them suitcases anyhow. So how ya like that, huh?"

The professor gritted his teeth. "Look here, the only thing we're taking that we didn't bring with us is a dusty old book that some former tenant forgot—"

Andy McDuff's mean, cold eyes narrowed at once. "A book, huh? Well, that's my property! You jist han' that book over if y' know what's good for ya!"

The professor's shoulders slumped. "That book is of no possible use to you," he said in a tired voice. "You cannot read it, and it's worthless as an antique. You can't make any money on it. The only one who might care about it at all is a scholar who specializes in old—"

"Shut up, fatty," snarled McDuff. "If ya ain't gonna listen

ta reason, I guess I'll jist hafta arrest th' three of ya. Ya like that, huh? Ya *want* these two kids ta have a jail record?"

Slowly the professor turned to look behind him at Johnny and Fergie. "No," he said in a low voice. "I can't let that happen." To Johnny's surprise, the professor winked at him. The old man set his suitcase down and opened it. He rummaged inside and took out a book-shaped parcel wrapped in brown paper. "Here you are," he said, his voice defeated. "Although what good it will do you, I cannot say."

"Good enough," sneered McDuff, taking the wrapped book. "Now git out o' here! An' don't ya ever come back."

"No fear of that," said the professor. He was already lashing his suitcase to the rear fender of his bike. "Come, gentlemen. We don't have a moment to lose."

A second later all three were on their bikes, pumping away. Behind them, Andy McDuff stood in the middle of the road, clutching the book to his chest. Johnny pedaled so hard that soon he was gasping for air. The sun had been down for more than half an hour, leaving just a smear of twilight over the Gulf to the west. The road was hard to see. The unpaved track was a gray glimmer, and the trees on either side were solid walls of blackness from which a million insects screeched and chattered.

But soon Johnny saw ahead the lights of the stores that clustered around the docks. A few moments later he leaned his bike against the side of the Sand Dollar Store, which was closed for the night. "If only the water taxi is still running," grunted the professor.

They were out of luck. No one was in the booth. They looked at each other for a few seconds. Fergie slapped at his face. "Great," he said. "We're gonna be stuck here all night, an' these mosquitoes are gonna drain us of every drop of blood. They'll find our poor, shriveled bodies in th' morning—"

"Oh, hush, Byron," said the professor. "You're just going to spook Johnny."

"He doesn't need to," said Johnny miserably. "I'm spooked already." The professor patted his shoulder, and then Johnny heard a man whistling "Hearts of Oak," an old British Navy song. "What's th' matter, folks?" asked a man's voice from the land side of the pier. "Need a lift?"

Johnny recognized the voice. It was Mr. Weatherall, from whom he and his dad had rented the *Swordfish*. "Hi, Mr. Weatherall," he said, stepping toward him. "We sure do! I'm Johnny Dixon. Remember me?"

Mr. Weatherall stepped beneath a light that threw a round puddle of yellow illumination at the head of the pier. "Why, of course! You an' your dad gave me a couple of nice fish. What's the trouble, folks?"

Professor Childermass said, "My good man, we were planning to spend a night on the island, but we got into a disagreement with the villain who runs Pirate's Cove. Now we need to get back to the mainland."

Mr. Weatherall chuckled and shook his head. "Andy McDuff, huh? Well, he's no friend of mine! Too big for his britches, if you ask me. Loves to boss people around. I'm just about to head home to Alachamokee myself, so if you three will climb into that green dinghy yonder, I'll be pleased to run you across."

The dinghy was small and rusty and smelled an awful lot like fish that had been out of the water too long, but Johnny was glad to crouch in the bow as Mr. Weatherall started the sputtering outboard motor. They zipped across the dark bay, winding between lighted buoys, and finished up at the same dock the water taxi had left from earlier that day. Professor Childermass tried to pay Mr. Weatherall, but the boat owner said, "Forget it. Anybody who don't get along with Andy McDuff is okay in my book. Y'all be careful, now, y' hear?"

Johnny, Fergie, and the professor hurried back up the dark alley to the parking lot where they had left their rental car. They all piled in, the professor started the engine, and with a loud screech of tires, they roared off toward Tallahassee.

"Suppose we can get an airplane tonight?" Fergie asked.

"I have no idea, Byron," returned the professor. "However, I want to be far away from Live Oak Key as quickly as possible."

"It's just too bad you had to give him the book," said Fergie.

"That is exactly why we need to get away," said the professor with a sharp, short laugh.

"What do you mean?" asked Johnny.

The professor chuckled again. "John, my boy, I am afraid that Mr. McDuff is going to be sorely disappointed. When Madam Lumiere warned us that someone was coming, I prepared for an emergency. I wrapped the book up in brown paper. But just to be on the safe side, I also wrapped up the Gideon Bible that was in my bedroom. And on the steps, I pulled what is technically known as the old switcheroo. I kept the mystic manuscript that nearly took Byron's fingers off, and I handed the Good Book over to Mr. McDuff. I hope he reads it! He's just the sort who could use some moral instruction!"

"Way to go, Prof!" crowed Fergie. "You know, you're gettin' *sneaky* in your old age!"

"Hah!" retorted the professor. "To quote Mr. Al Jolson, Byron, 'You ain't seen nothin' yet.' Why, back in World War One, when I was in Army Intelligence, I pulled off some snazzy tricks that left the enemy wondering what had hit them! I..."

Johnny relaxed with a sigh. As the car sped north through the Florida night, he held on to a little spark of hope. He did not understand how, and he did not know why, but the magical book might be the key to saving his father's life. Johnny had been living on his nerves for days. He had been so high strung that he had slept very little, and he had eaten far less than he needed to keep going. Now he felt on the verge of collapse. Clutching tight to that one little gleam of hope, he fell asleep as the car rocked through the night and the professor's voice droned on.

A few hours after he had stopped the three at the foot of the steps, Mr. Andy McDuff unlocked the door of a fishing shack on the south tip of Live Oak Key. He carried a flashlight, which he used to locate a candle. Then he lit the candle, and used it to light another dozen.

The thirteen candles were all black. They illuminated a strange room, which took up the whole interior of the square little house. It measured thirteen feet wide, thirteen feet long, and thirteen feet from floor to ceiling.

The room had no windows. The walls, floor, and ceiling were all painted a flat black. It was the color of midnight in the middle of the most forsaken swamp on earth.

On the floor was a circle drawn in a vivid blood red. The circle held a pentagram, a five-pointed star. Each point of the star had a different Hebrew letter inscribed in it, and words written in the unknown script used in the magic book filled the spaces between the points.

McDuff looked at his wristwatch. It was one minute to midnight. He went to the center of the pentagram and knelt. He took the wrapped book from inside his jacket and laid it on the floor in front of him. By the wavering yellow light of the candles he watched the minute hand of his watch crawl closer and closer to the twelve.

When the time was exactly midnight, McDuff raised his hands and held them straight out, palms up. "Nyarlat-Hotep!" he intoned, his voice deep and booming, very different from its normal speaking pitch. "Hear me, O spirit of Nyarlat-Hotep! Hear me, Ancient One! Attend me, Master Who Was and Will Be! Lo, thy servant has done thy bidding!"

The candles did not go completely out, but the light in the room changed. Each flame burned blue and dim, and the darkness became almost thick enough to feel.

A purring, inhuman voice said, "Hast thou spilled the blood of mine enemies? Hast thou put them to sword and flame?"

"I found the book!" said McDuff in a frightened, whiny tone. "The one with a mind of its own! The one that could open the doorway! It got away from you, but I found it and brought it back! You can take it to your world, O Lurker on the Threshold! Then no one on earth can stand against you!

You can make your sacrifice and gain your power over your world and over this one!"

A darker shape gathered in the air before McDuff, as if a charcoal-gray fog were collecting. It had the vague shape of a skull, and it seemed to wear a demonic triumphant grin. From its dark sockets blazed two red eyes, glaring and filled with hate. "The Grimoire of Frascati!" thundered the voice. "Had I gained full strength when I entered the mind of the sleeping mortal Harrison Dixon, I would have used his body to destroy that gateway! Show me! Show me the book now!"

"Here it is!" With hands shaking as if he had a terrible case of palsy, Andy McDuff unwrapped the brown paper. "I hope you'll reward me for this," he said. "I hadda fight three big tough men t'—"

He broke off in confusion. He held in his hands a black book. On the cover in gilt script were the words "Holy Bible."

The silence was deafening.

McDuff dropped the book to the floor. He scrambled to his feet. "No," he said wildly, throwing up his arms to shield his head. "No! It wasn't my fault! It wasn't—"

He exploded into a ball of fire.

As dawn rose the next morning, two fishermen saw wreaths of gray smoke drifting from the south end of Live Oak Key. They rowed ashore to investigate and found the ashes of an old fishing shack. It had burned completely. In the center of the ruin, they were horrified to see a blackened human skeleton. The intense heat had shriveled the bones and had reduced some of the ribs to gray powder. "Look at that," one of the men said. "Wonder who it coulda been."

The other man shook his head. "Only way they'll be able t' tell is th' teeth," he said. "Prob'ly some drunk come in here t' sleep an' set himself on fire with a cigarette or sumpin'. Say, don't ol' Andy McDuff own this place?"

"Yup," the first man said. "And won't he be mad when he finds out somebody burned it to th' ground! Joe, what's this here?"

He stooped to pick up something from the ashes. "It's a

Bible," Joe said, looking over his friend's shoulder. "Ain't it burned?"

"Not even scorched," the first man said. "If this don't beat all."

"Well, we better get on into the settlement," Joe said. "I expect ol' Andy will want to know about this as soon as possible."

"Yeah," his friend agreed. "I guess we better not touch nothin'." He put the Bible carefully back on the ground, and the two left it with the gilt title gleaming in the morning sun.

CHAPTER TEN

At noon that day Johnny, Fergie, the professor, Dr. Coote, and Father Thomas Higgins met in the parsonage of St. Michael's Church. Father Higgins had returned from his conference the day before, and the others spent half an hour explaining to him what had happened. He frowned and nodded as he listened. He was a tough-looking priest, six feet tall with a square, grizzled jaw and bushy eyebrows set in a permanent scowl. Johnny knew he was a brave man. Father Higgins had served as an Army chaplain in the Philippines during World War II, and he had seen some heavy action. Despite his forbidding appearance, he had been a good friend to Johnny, and his kind heart occasionally showed through as a warm twinkle in his green eyes.

When Professor Childermass finished his quick summary, the priest shook his head. "Incredible," he said. "Roderick, I know you too well to think that you're mistaken about any of this. But if anyone else had told me such a wild story, I'd wonder about his sanity. And what do you have to say, Dr. Coote? Can you tell us anything about this strange book?"

Dr. Coote coughed. "Of course, I have not had time to examine it thoroughly," he said. "And I've had only a limited time to search for answers in my books. Roderick called me from Tallahassee last night, and I drove down to Boston to meet him at the airport at two in the morning. I spent all the rest of last night looking over this, um, odd artifact."

"Confound it, Charley, the man asked you a question," grumbled Professor Childermass, who had not had much sleep either. "Can you tell us anything at all about this blasted book?"

"Yes, yes, I'm getting to that," said Dr. Coote mildly. "Well, the book superficially resembles the Voynich Manuscript I told Roderick and Johnny about a few days ago. However, the lettering is very different, and the pictures are not the same. The paper is a good grade of vellum. From the type of vellum and the degree to which the inks have faded, I would guess that the manuscript dates from no later than the sixteenth century, and possibly from much earlier, depending on how well it has been kept. I know for certain that it was re-bound in 1883."

"How do you know that?" asked the priest.

Dr. Coote opened the book to the inside of the back cover. He pointed to a little pasted-in label, barely visible between the spine and the back flyleaf, that read "Southern Star Bindery, Jacksonville, Florida, 1883."

"Something I overlooked," admitted the professor. "But that isn't the important thing, Higgy. The book is some kind of gateway between this world and the infernal world. Or if not to the haunts that Dante explored with the ghost of Virgil, at least to *some* spiritual realm. That's what Brewster told us."

"And where is Brewster?" asked Father Higgins.

Johnny pulled the thunderbird figure from his pocket. "He's not talking again," he said.

"He kinda clams up sometimes," added Fergie.

"Irritating fowl," groused the professor. "I don't know how to force him to squawk, unless maybe we try some kind of super-duper Ouija board."

"Try it, Whiskers," said a faint, faraway voice. "Try it and see how far it gets you!"

Father Higgins blinked. "Well, Roderick, since I haven't heard of you taking up ventriloquism, I presume that is a spirit's voice. Brewster, I take it?"

"Brewster," said the professor. "And high time too!"

"Extraordinary," remarked Dr. Coote. "This occurrence reminds me of Jeanne d'Arc, who heard voices—"

"Can it, Charley," said the professor. "Brewster! We rescued this terrible tome from Florida, just as you advised us, and it took some doing. Now tell us about it, blast you! Let us know what we've got our mitts on!"

"It is a gateway," came the irascible voice of Brewster. "Just like I told you. Look, my friends, I have to explain a few things and I have to be quick about it. First off, Father Higgins, my world is *not* Hades or Purgatory or even Limbo. It's a universe of spirits that is different from those other places. It has always existed, as far as we spirits know— anyhow, none of us can remember a time when it didn't exist. Our natural laws are different from those of your world. You'd call them magic. Some of your human sorcerers and magicians have had glimpses of this realm in trances or dreams. Occasionally, one of them would put these visions down in books of magic lore. Sometimes spirits from my side have even helped them out."

"And sometimes," said Professor Childermass, "some of you have masqueraded as gods! Right, Horus?"

"Aw, lay off me," said Brewster. "So I get lonesome and want some human company once in a millennium or thereabouts! So my friends and I used to spend some hours in Egyptian temples, passing the time of day with priests and worshipers. Ya gonna sue me for showing up and demonstrating a little magic power now and again, Whiskers?"

"Please," said Father Higgins. "Look, ah, Brewster, we want to help Major Dixon. What can you tell me about him?"

The thin voice became even softer. "He is here."

"No," Fergie said in surprise. "He's in th' hospital."

"Only his body," returned Brewster's voice. "The spirit side of him is a captive. The one we call Nyarlat-Hotep is trying to cast him into such despair that he will die, body and soul."

"Why?" asked Johnny, his voice anguished. "What did Dad ever do to him?"

"Understand," replied Brewster, "that we spirits can occasionally enter your world. Nyarlat-Hotep first walked among you as a man many thousands of your years ago. He delights in pain and fear. They make him stronger. When he first came to earth, he took human form. He was so powerful that soon he dominated a whole continent full of frightened people. And he cast that continent into the sea, just to feed on the grief, the terror, and the agony of a million dying souls!"

"Lost Atlantis," whispered Dr. Coote. "Oh, merciful heavens!"

"Yes, but didn't old Gnarly die in the same deluge?" asked the professor. "I mean, it stands to reason! How can you drown a whole continent and escape high and dry yourself?"

"The body died," explained Brewster, "but the evil spirit lived on! It returned here! The Law is that when that happens, when a spirit returns to our world from earth, it must drink the Water of Forgetfulness—"

"Lethe," suggested Dr. Coote. "Mythology speaks of a river called Lethe, whose water makes anyone who drinks of it forget his whole past."

"Bingo," said Brewster. "But Nyarlat-Hotep broke the Law. He has never taken his drink from Lethe. Even worse, he keeps trying to force his way through to earth. Three hundred years ago, he took the body and appearance of the pirate Damon Boudron. We tried spells to bring him back, but he fought us. He sacrificed twelve humans in various gory ways so that he could remain on earth and repeat his coup. Except this time he wanted to wipe out the whole human race! Some of us on this side fouled up his plan at the last minute by causing an earthquake and drowning Boudron's body again—but Nyarlat-Hotep's spirit fled back here and hid itself. Even worse, it brought the skeleton of Boudron with it, so it is partly spirit and partly material. It does not belong completely either to our world or to yours, so it is hard to fight. Now it is trying to make that last sacrifice, unlucky number thirteen. If that happens, *your* world will be doomed, and *ours* will fall under Nyarlat-Hotep's cruel rule forever!"

"Why Dad?" asked Johnny, his voice shaky. "Why couldn't he have picked on anybody else?"

"Just anyone won't do," snapped Brewster. "The sacrifice has to be someone who is a brave warrior. His will to live must be utterly broken so he gives himself as a willing sacrifice. And he must be completely, eternally destroyed, both body and soul forever!"

"That's blasphemous!" exclaimed Father Higgins. "We have to stop this now!"

"But—" put in Dr. Coote in his mild, reedy voice, "but how, exactly, are we to do that? Can, ah, Brewster offer any advice?"

The voice of Brewster was becoming fainter and fainter. "You will have to come through to this side," it said. "You must put the enchanted book in a holy place. Gather around it. Command it to open the way, and then pass through."

"Hang it," thundered the professor. "Why are *you* so helpful? What is your concern in all this?"

For a few seconds it seemed as if Brewster would not answer. Then, in a small voice, he said, "Nyarlat-Hotep and I are, well, like brothers. We were created at the same time, back in the days of ancient Egypt. I could have stopped him when he first turned evil, but I did nothing. Now I must make up for that. Hurry! Time is short! I will wait on the other side! I can't speak to you anymore now..." The sound faded until it was as soft as a mosquito's droning hum, and then it was gone.

They all looked at each other. "A holy place," said Father Higgins slowly. "I suppose that means the church. I'll get some holy water, my breviary, and—"

Professor Childermass held up his hand. "No, Higgy. I don't think you should."

"Why not?" asked the priest. His face flushed with annoyance. "Rod, I'll have you know that I am not afraid—"

"I know you aren't," said the professor. "But I don't want to jump down this rabbit hole without leaving someone at the other end! So I think you should stay, and of course I'd never dream of asking you, Charley, to come along. Your legs aren't very strong, you know. I am certainly going." He was holding his Knights of Columbus sword in its scabbard. With a defiant look, he stood up, unfastened his belt, and hung the sword on it. "I am going," he repeated meaningfully, "and I am going armed!"

Johnny swallowed hard. "I have to go," he said. "It's for my dad."

Fergie beamed from ear to ear. "John baby, when I first met you at Boy Scout camp, I never dreamed we'd be doin' stuff like fightin' ghosts and zippin' off to La-La Land. But ya know what? I like it! Count me in, Prof."

And so it was settled. They took the strange book into St. Michael's Church and set it before the altar. Father Higgins blessed the professor, Johnny, and Fergie—even though Fergie made a face and said, "Aw, Father Higgins, you know I'm a Baptist. Ya sure this is gonna take?"

The priest smiled weakly. "Let's say it's like giving chicken soup to a man with a broken leg, Fergie. It can't hurt!"

Solemnly, the professor, Johnny, and Fergie shook hands with Dr. Coote and Father Higgins. Then Professor Childermass said, "Are we ready, troops?"

"Sure," said Fergie. "Bring on th' ghosts!"

Johnny could not speak. He had a huge lump in his throat, and his knees were shaking. But he managed to nod.

They stood around the book. Professor Childermass cleared his throat and said, "Open the gateway! We command it!"

With a flop! the book opened itself. The pages showed drawings of awful-looking plants with the faces of tortured, screaming people in the center of the petals. Johnny wondered if he had the courage to go through with this. He wondered if everyone would call him a coward if he backed out.

But then he looked at the professor's face. He could see that Professor Childermass was pale with dread. Still, the old man's chin was set in firm resolve. And Fergie kept swallowing.

We're all afraid, Johnny realized. He knew in that instant that, whatever happened, he had to carry out his part. They had to depend on each other. If necessary, they had to borrow courage from each other. They had to do it for Johnny's dad.

The professor glowered at the motionless book. "Open the gateway!" he thundered. "By all that is holy, I command it! Come on, you rotten sheaf of worm-eaten paper! Let us through. I dare you! I *double* dare you!"

Something began to happen. A whirling gray cloud started to form in the air above the open book. At first it was only a puff of vapor the size of a baseball. It grew and grew until it was ten feet tall and five feet broad. It looked like a section of a tornado, all lashing, dark clouds, and eerie flashes of what could be purple lightning. A hollow, groaning voice said: "ENTER, MORTALS!"

"Angels and ministers of grace defend us!" mumbled the professor. Then he straightened so that his back was like a ramrod. Johnny had a glimpse of him as he must have looked in World War I, as a dashing, heroic Army officer. "Forward, march!" barked the professor.

They all took a step toward the center. Johnny entered the cloud. He tried to scream, but an infernal wind whipped the cry right out of his throat. He felt himself falling and falling. It seemed to go on forever, that terrible plunge into darkness.

"Good Lord in heaven," gasped Dr. Coote as his three friends stepped into the cloud and simply faded from sight, as if their bodies had dissolved. "It worked!"

"Watch out!" screamed Father Higgins, grabbing the older man's shoulders and dragging him back.

They both yelled in dismay. The book itself flapped and fluttered and then leaped up into the swirling cloud. The cloud swelled for an instant, then immediately shrank to nothing. A thunderclap shook the whole church, rattling the stained-glass windows and making both men stagger.

Father Higgins shouted, "No!"

Dr. Coote looked at the empty floor. "My stars! The

book—it... it's gone too," he stammered. "My heavens, Father Higgins—*how will they get back?*"

Father Higgins could only give him a sick look. That was a question no man alive could answer.

CHAPTER ELEVEN

Johnny lost all sense of direction. He had the sensation of terrific speed, of air rushing past him, but he had absolutely no sense of *up* or *down*. Everything around him was dark. It was as if he had been launched into the darkest region of the universe, where not even a star shared his loneliness. He felt as if the vast nothingness around him were trying to tear at his mind, to rip away his sanity and his identity until he would be nothing but a bundle of terrors.

He tried to shout, but his voice made no sound in this terrible void. He could neither see nor hear the professor or Fergie. A horrible thought struck him: What if *they* had chickened out? What if, at the last moment, they had stopped short of the whirling gray cloud? What if he was truly and absolutely alone?

He tried to pray, but words would not form themselves in his mind. Seconds may have flown past, or hours may have dragged by. Time had no meaning. The only reality was the endless fall and rising horror.

And then, somehow, Johnny was standing. Standing on a gray, rolling plain that stretched endlessly away from him in all directions. He gasped in air, and heard the sound of his gasp. The surface he was standing on felt springy, more like firm rubber than earth, and yet things grew from it. Leprous fungi sent up curved sprouts, like the fingers of dead men. Here and there, twisted trees held their leafless branches up, as if begging for mercy from the dark sky.

The sky. Johnny looked up. A disk of dark gray cloud was overhead, reaching practically all the way to the horizon. There dim, washed-out light marked what could be a glimpse of sky. All around the edge of this strange world, it was the same. The lid of cloud ceased a little above the horizon, letting that bleary, bloodless light leak in.

Johnny had never felt so alone in all his life. "Professor?" he yelled as loud as he could. The word died with no hint of echo. "Fergie?" No answer. No sound at all, not even wind.

Johnny was lost and terrified. "What should I do?" he asked, not even hoping for a response. Which way should he go? Where were his friends?

Johnny had a fleeting moment when he wondered if he had actually gone insane, if all this was some crazy nightmare in his brain. Maybe he was lying helpless in some mental ward right this instant—

"There you are!"

Johnny squeaked in alarm and spun around. Standing a few feet behind him was the strangest being he had ever seen. It looked like a little man only about three feet high, except that his body was completely covered with black feathers. He had the head of a hawk, with a down-curved beak, hooded, ferocious-looking eyes, and a proud expression. He wore a kind of kilt of white linen, golden bracelets and armbands, a strange double golden crown, and golden sandals on his feet, which, despite their feathers, looked human.

"B-Brewster?" Johnny asked.

The little creature bowed. "One and the same. Good weather and good fortune my specialties! I appear at religious rites, spring festivals, harvest feasts, and bar mitzvahs! Well, not the bar mitzvahs so much, to tell the truth. Are you all right?"

"I think so," Johnny said. "This is a terrible place."

Brewster looked offended, or as offended as a being with a bird's head could manage. "Hey!" he said. "This isn't the *nice* part, okay? Give me a break. What if you popped up on earth for the first time in your life in the middle of Death Valley, or on the Greenland ice cap? They wouldn't look so hot either, right?"

"I'm sorry," said Johnny. "I didn't mean to—"

"Don't sweat it," Brewster said. "Johnny, this is a part of

our world we call the Blighted Lands. It doesn't look like much, but I don't think there's anything around that can hurt you. Now I have to go round up Whiskers and Fergie, and I need to keep tabs on you. So you go over to that palm tree there and sit very quietly beneath it. I'll be back in two shakes of a poltergeist's tail."

"Palm tree?" asked Johnny. "Where?"

"That one right there," said Brewster, pointing. "And tell it to keep its hands to itself!" He disappeared with a soft pop.

Johnny walked slowly toward the tree, though it didn't look like any palm tree he had ever seen. It was more like one of the live oaks down in Florida, but leafless, its twisted branches looking tortured and stark. As he approached it, Johnny saw how it got its name. Each branch ended in a hand—a hand with spread-out, clutching fingers made of twigs. These began to strain toward him, clenching and unclenching as if eager to seize him and tear him to bits.

"K-keep your hands to yourself!" faltered Johnny, trying to sound big and bold but only succeeding in sounding half scared out of his wits.

The strange tree quivered as if in frustration. The branches folded up, crossing the trunk. It looked like one of those Indian idols with about eight arms having a grumpy day. Nervously, Johnny edged up to the trunk and sat down on the strange, spongy ground. He wondered what would happen next.

Splash!

Fergie plunged feet first into water. At least, it *splashed* like water. It had a gunky, greasy, disgusting feel to it, though, and it was as warm and slimy as blood. He kept his eyes and mouth clamped shut, squeezed his nose with the fingers of his left hand, and struck off kicking for the surface. He opened his eyes to find himself floating in an empty sea. The water was thick and sluggish, like oil. It had a sick gray color shot through with veins of red and purple. Slow, ponderous waves spread out from the spot where Fergie had landed.

He began to tread water. Above him was a purple sky of broken clouds, with one angry red star burning far away. Everything was in a kind of half-light. With growing desperation Fergie saw that he was alone, and that the sea went right on to the horizon. He was a good swimmer, but he could not stay afloat forever.

And then, to his vast relief, he saw an island nearby. A low, humped island, bare of any trees, but not too far away for him to swim the distance. He struggled to untie his sneakers, got them off, knotted the laces together, and slung them around his neck. Then he struck out in a long, powerful crawl stroke.

Fergie hated the feel of that otherworldly liquid against his face. He tried to gulp air only when his mouth was well clear of the surface. Closer and closer he came to the island. When he was a few feet away, Fergie dropped his feet and felt for the bottom. He sank seven or eight feet and then kicked back to the surface.

Weird, he thought. The beach must have a drop-off like nobody's business! He swam the ten or eleven feet to the rocky island, then dragged himself up until he was out of the water. He lay there gasping and hugging the ground. Then he climbed up the domed, greenish-blue rock on all fours until he was at the summit. All around him was the empty sea. Except for scraggly red tufts of what looked like wire grass, the island had no vegetation. It was maybe a quarter of a mile in diameter.

Fergie noticed something else. Everything was quiet. He had never been to an ocean, lake, or even pond that didn't have *some* sound going on around it: the chirping of crickets, the swash of waves, the whisper of wind. But this place was absolutely dead silent.

Dead.

Fergie wondered where in the world—or out of it— Johnny and the professor had wound up. Had they plunged into this ocean too? If so—

Fear climbed Fergie's spine. Johnny was not a very good swimmer. The professor was over seventy years old. How long could they live in this bizarre sea? Had they already drowned? Were their bodies drifting down, down, to endless depths?

Fergie leaped to his feet, seized with an impulse to run away. Run—that was a laugh! Run *where?* Despite his dread, Fergie laughed at himself. "Byron Q. Ferguson," he said aloud, "you can run in little circles until you die of exhaustion or go nuts with th' howling heebie-jeebies! Great choice, huh?" He stood there dripping, wondering what to do next. In all the stories the hero would go and explore the island. But what was the point? From up here Fergie could *see* the whole island, and there wasn't anything to explore!

"Oh, boy," he said. "I've landed in a load of trouble for sure this time."

"You said it, Bright Eyes," came a familiar voice.

Fergie turned around and somehow instantly recognized the little creature that stood just behind him. "Brewster!" hollered Fergie. "Where th' devil have you been? An' where's Johnny?"

"Keep your hair on," Brewster said. "He's okay. That's two down! Now I have to get you to Johnny, and then I've got to locate Whiskers. Okay, I'm going to fly you. Don't be scared."

"Hah!" said Fergie. "Let's take off. The sooner the better!"

Though he had no wings, Brewster rose up into the air. Somehow, and Fergie had no idea of exactly how, Brewster became a gigantic falcon, flapping powerful wings to keep aloft. "Hold still," he said. He came behind Fergie and slipped his talons around the boy's shoulders. They grasped beneath Fergie's armpits. With no apparent effort, he picked Fergie up until his toes dangled a few inches above the peak of the island's dome. "Hmm," said Brewster thoughtfully. "I think I can manage it. You're not as heavy as I thought. All right. Up, up, and away, as Superduperman says in the funny papers!"

Fergie caught his breath. It was like being in a runaway

elevator. They shot straight up, then hovered there. Looking down past his big dangling feet, Fergie saw the round island. "Not much of a vacation spot," he grunted.

"You're not just whistling 'Dixie,' " said Brewster. Then he shouted, "Okay, Poseidon! I got him now!"

To Fergie's astonishment, the whole island rose and tilted. An enormous face looked up at them—the face of a manlike being with greenish, fishlike features. "Glad to help!" came a glubby reply from the creature's blubbery lips, and then the head submerged.

"Oh, wow," Fergie said as Brewster began to swoop through the air with him. "This is a crazy place!"

Professor Childermass tried to take a squelchy step. Thick, cold, clammy mud clutched and sucked at his legs. He groaned and fell forward in slow motion. Then he caught himself and forced his aching legs to take another step.

"No-man's-land," he said, shivering. He had fallen into a nightmare landscape. Tangles of briars, curled like concertina wire, rolled across an expanse of splintered trees and gaping craters containing stagnant, stinking green water. A cold drizzle began to fall from the gray, ragged sky. The professor had seen something very much like this before in his life, back in World War I.

That war had been fought between armies that hunkered down in trenches facing each other. The ground between the two armies was called no-man's-land. Shells and bombs ripped it to shreds, and the endless rain mixed with human blood to create a dreadful mud. Professor Childermass had entered the Army as a cook. Serving in the front lines had been appalling, and when he performed an act of bravery and was offered a battlefield promotion as a reward, he took the opportunity like a shot. He became an intelligence officer, working behind enemy lines. Though he faced the threat of capture and torture at every moment, he preferred that to the hideous living death of the trenches and of no-man's-land.

"It isn't the same," he told himself, grunting. "Not the

same at all. For one thing, there's no sound of five-nine shells whistling in. And no whomps of poison-gas canisters bursting open to choke the life out of you! Keep moving, Captain Childermass!"

He slogged painfully to a little rise. It was at least more solid than the sea of mud that lay all about. The briars were bad there, though, springy coils of vines with nasty sharp hooks that latched into his skin and tore painful gashes. He swore between his teeth and painfully worked himself free, all the while wondering what had happened to Johnny and Fergie. "Dear God," he breathed. "What have I gotten those boys into?" He felt chilled to the bone, and as weary as death. "John Michael!" he shouted at the top of his lungs. "Byron! Where are you?"

The only answer was the dreary, endless hiss of rain. Professor Childermass took off his glasses, tried to scrub them dry, and put them back on again. He might as well have tried to look through the bottoms of two pop bottles. "Brewster!" he yelled. "Hang it, Horus! Where are you? You promised to help, you chicken-headed excuse for a squidgy-nosed old idol!"

"I'm here, I'm here," said Brewster. "Give me a hand up, would you?"

Professor Childermass dropped to his knees and looked over the steep side of the rise. A feathery black creature was creeping up—or trying to.

"About time!" roared the professor, reaching down and grabbing him by the scruff of the neck. He swung Brewster up, finding him surprisingly light. "Where are John and Byron? What—"

"Please," groaned Brewster, slapping his feathered hands to the sides of his head where his ears would have been if he'd had any. "You three wound up in different places, that's all. You're all fine."

The professor scraped a handful of mud off his trousers and tossed it at Brewster's feet, where it landed with a squelch. "You call *this* fine?" he snarled. "You obviously are using some definition of the word with which I am not familiar!"

"You're alive and in one piece," said Brewster hastily. "And, what is even better, you haven't attracted the attention of Nyarlat-Hotep. Yet. But that can't last for long. Now, are you ready to join your friends?"

"What do I do?" asked the professor crabbily. "Tap my heels together three times and say 'There's no place like the spirit world'?"

"That won't be necessary," replied Brewster sulkily. "If you can walk in this direction, the going gets easier. You can find Johnny and Fergie if you just don't give up."

"Walk through this?" demanded the professor with a gesture that took in the endless mud. "Maybe when I was twenty! I've tried to keep myself in shape, but I've got old-geezer legs!"

"Easy, easy," said Brewster. "There is a path through the mire. I'll go first, and you follow in my footsteps. It's yucky and slippery, but not hard. Ready? Or are those old-geezer legs going to fold up under you like a couple of bamboo umbrellas?"

"You sawed-off smart aleck," snapped the professor. "Anywhere you can go, I can go faster! Want to race? Want to put your money where your beak is?"

"Come on, Grandpa," responded Brewster, hopping down into the bog with a curious birdlike motion. "See if you can keep up!"

The professor had not been boasting. He *had* kept himself in good shape, exercising and going for long, long walks. He had even given up smoking not long before, and now he was grateful for his increased lung power. Here, though, with lardy clots of slick mud underfoot, he stumbled and staggered for what felt like hours. At last the ground rose, becoming gray and rubbery, but dry. An exhausted Professor Childermass stumbled on, following a silent Brewster.

Something ahead. The professor was so tired that at first he muttered, "Machine-gun nest? Pillbox? Got to get word back to headquarters." Then, with a shock, he snapped out of it as he saw Fergie and Johnny standing beneath an odd-looking tree. With a shout of pure joy he dashed past Brewster, ran to the two boys, and threw his arms around both of them. "I'm so glad to see you safe!" he roared, ruffling their hair.

"Quiet," cautioned Brewster, hurrying up. "Quiet, or they won't be safe for long!" He looked around nervously. "Now everyone settle down," he said. "You have to know a thing or three before you try to tackle Nyarlat-Hotep. And I don't know how long we've got before he sends his minions."

"Minions?" asked Johnny anxiously.

"You don't want to know," Brewster said fervently. "Believe me, you don't want to know."

And then he told them anyway.

CHAPTER TWELVE

"Have you ever heard of Pythagoras?" asked Brewster, who kept glancing around.

Fergie scratched his head. "Sure," he said. "The square of the hypotenuse of a right triangle is equal to the sums of the squares of the other two sides. That's the Pythagorean theorem."

The professor, who had been trying to scrape some of the mud from his shoes and his legs, straightened with a grunt. "True enough, Byron, but I believe our friend here is referring to another idea of that ancient Greek gentleman. If memory serves, Pythagoras also spoke of the transmigration of souls."

Fergie looked baffled. "The trans-whatzis? Is that like a subway system?"

"Not exactly," said the professor. "It's the notion that when a person dies, his soul doesn't fly to glory or sink down to eternal punishment, but is reborn."

"Like reincarnation," Johnny said. "Lots of ancient people believed in that."

"Yes," said Professor Childermass, wagging a finger, "but this is not the kind of reincarnation where a person dies in, say India, and immediately comes to life again as a baby in Peru. No, indeed! Pythagoras thought that one's soul would either go *up* or *down* the scale of existence, according to one's deeds in life. If you had been a good little boy and always ate every bit of your spinach and never, ever told a lie, you might be reborn as a prince. But if you had been naughty, you could come back as some nasty animal—or even an earthworm or a dung beetle."

"Yuck," said Fergie, making a face.

"Yes," said Brewster quickly. "Well, we spirits are subject to that Law. If—and I say *if*—we get ourselves somehow born into your world, with a material body, then when that body dies, we're supposed to be reborn in a better or worse one. But Nyarlat-Hotep is disobeying that Law. He's still using the body of Damon Boudron."

"But he died over two hundred and sixty years ago!" Johnny said.

Brewster's expressive beak gave an impression of disgust. "I didn't say it was attractive!" he announced.

"I don't get it," said Fergie. "If this Nasty-Hotbox guy is breakin' so many of your rules, why don't you throw him in th' hoosegow? That big fellow I saw in the ocean should be able to do it."

Brewster looked ashamed. "Some of us are too scared to try," he muttered. "And some others are even on his side. Those are his minions, terrible creatures who, unlike the rest of us, do not take their forms from earthly ideas. They've never really liked the earth. Every generation, some wizard or sorceress tries to latch on to a spirit or two and enslave us to do their will. It never works out, frankly, but the magicians keep trying. Some of us have been grumbling that it would be better just to let everyone on earth perish and be done with it once and for all. That's one reason the other spirits have not made war on Nyarlat-Hotep." He hung his head. "But most of all," he said in a quiet whisper, "we can't do anything about his body. It comes from *your* world. Only somebody from your world can destroy it."

"So how do we do that?" asked the professor, angrily rattling his sword in its scabbard. "If you'd warned me, I would've tried to round up a couple of grenades or a flamethrower. As it is, we are woefully under-equipped!"

"I don't *know* how to deal with him," said Brewster. "If I did, I wouldn't have asked you guys here. But as I see it, you can do this only one way. The key is to get Nyarlot-Hotep to swallow some of the water of Lethe. Even one tiny drop will make him forget all his plans. He won't even know who he is. Then if you can knock his block off—I mean literally bop his bean right off his shoulders—then the Law of our world will crash down on him. All his evil deeds will slam him to another form. You might have to deal with him as the other form too. If you can destroy that, he'll come back as something else. When he gets weak enough, we can deal with him."

"Okay," said Fergie. "Take a little off the top, huh? And he's more'n two hundred an' fifty years old? That shouldn't be too hard."

"He has powers at his bidding," said Brewster sadly. "He is the master of fears and darkness! He will send your worst nightmares against you! And if he overpowers you here, he will destroy your bodies. Your enslaved souls will become part of his wretched army forever."

"World without end, amen," finished the professor. "Stow it, Birdy. We'll take our chances and stand up against that moldering mountebank. How about it, gentlemen? One for all, and all for one?"

"You said it, Prof," answered Fergie.

"I'm in," said Johnny. "Anything to save Dad."

"All right," said the professor. "Now for the sixty-four thousand dollar question: Where do we find this creature?"

Brewster shivered. "We are on the outskirts of his kingdom," he said. "I can take the form of a falcon and fly ahead. If you will follow me, you will soon be within sight of his Palace of Dreadful Night."

"How far is it?" asked Fergie.

Brewster shook his head. "I can't tell you that, exactly. Nyarlat-Hotep's domain is past your boundaries of time and space. It may seem hundreds of miles to you, or you may find it with your next step. It may seem to take you a hundred years or a heartbeat."

"Wha-a-at?" asked the professor, sounding like a cranky old rooster.

"It's true!" exclaimed Brewster. "By your standards, time may not even run the same way. You may be living backward, or, or—"

"Or inside out and upside down and sideways and six ways to Sunday," grumped the professor. "All right, all right! If we're to get nothing but metaphysical mystification from you, include me out of the conversation. Less talk, more walk! Show us the way, and we will follow."

"First," said Brewster, "the waters of Lethe. This way."

So began the weirdest journey Johnny had ever taken. The springy, rubbery ground seemed to shift and flow underfoot with some horrible life of its own. At one point they saw a group of people coming toward them, three exhausted-looking, staggering figures. "Don't look at them," warned Brewster, spiraling down from the air. Johnny and the others averted their eyes as they passed the limping trio. A year later—or was it only a moment?—he, Fergie, and the professor stood on the bank of a sluggish, winding stream, perhaps ten feet across. The water was the midnight color of India ink, but its surface sent back no reflection.

"This is it?" asked Professor Childermass in a weary voice.

Brewster, who had been soaring ahead of them, descended in a graceful circle. He was a falcon when in the air, but the second his toes touched ground, he became a three-foot tall man with the head of a falcon again. "This is it," he said. "Careful! You don't want to swallow even a drop of this stuff, or everything you know about who you are will fly out of your head like a bee out of a hive!"

"I didn't bring my canteen," said the professor sarcastically. "How do you propose we carry this water?"

Brewster reached into his belt and produced three odd-shaped little vials. One was blue, one red, and one yellow. They were tiny bottles, large enough to hold only half an ounce or so apiece. The blue one was diamond shaped, the red one oval, and the yellow one a perfect little cube. "Careful," warned Brewster again. "Try not to get any on you."

Fergie took the blue bottle and went first. Gripping it between finger and thumb, he dipped the neck below the surface. He lifted it and they all saw that it was half full of the water. Brewster supplied a long, thin cork, and Fergie popped it into the bottle. Then, as if curious, he licked his finger.

"Fergie!" shouted Johnny, alarmed.

Fergie staggered. Professor Childermass grabbed him. "Byron! Are you all right?"

"Huh?" Fergie blinked his eyes. "Fergie? Byron? I know not these names. I am—I am—who am I?" He blinked twice. "I don't remember a thing."

"Fergie!" wailed Johnny. "Why did you do that?"

"Fergie?" asked Fergie, looking completely flummoxed. "I know of no Fergie. And who are you strange people?" He pointed at Horus. "Is that Daffy Du—"

"Watch it, kid!" snapped Brewster.

The professor, sounding desperate, asked, "Brewster, there must be an antidote for—"

"There is none," answered the little creature sadly.

Fergie's face showed absolute bewilderment. "Who am I? Who could I be? I have to think."

Johnny's heart leaped as recognition dawned in Fergie's clouded eyes. "Do you remember?" he asked eagerly.

Beaming, Fergie nodded. A beatific smile spread over his face. "Of course! I remember now! I'm the King of the May!" He threw back his head and brayed with laughter. "Man, you should see your faces! Didn't you guys notice that I held the bottle in my *right* hand, but I put the finger of my *left* hand in my mouth?"

The professor snorted in disgust. "Stop fooling around!" he growled. "John, give me your bottle. I am not about to risk another scare like that one!" Carefully the old man half filled the remaining two bottles. He looked at the outside of each before corking it. "Remarkable," he said. "Not a drop clings to the glass. Most unusual water."

"What did you expect?" asked Brewster in his raspy, grouchy way. "Now come on. We must journey to the Pass of Shadows. And I hope it is still open. No one knows what Nyarlat-Hotep has been up to in these deserted lands."

So began yet another leg of the strange pilgrimage. Johnny felt as if he were dreaming. There was that same quality of unreality he had experienced in nightmares, where at one moment he would be in one place, and in seemingly the very next moment another place completely different. Not long after they left the river, they saw three figures staggering toward them. Brewster descended and shouted, "Don't look!" Johnny and the others averted their eyes—

"Oh, my gosh!" exclaimed Fergie. "We just passed *us*! That was us, on the way *toward* the river!"

"Space and time have no meaning here," said Brewster, rising again.

Johnny's teeth chattered. How could he be in two places at the same time? When he tried to think about it, he felt as if he were on the edge of madness. He shoved the thought far down in his mind.

As if in a hallucination Johnny noticed outlandish scenes and otherworldly plants. He saw vast mountains that rose abruptly from level plains, their steep sides as smooth as glass, making them regular cones. Later he gawked at daisies the size of trees, their enormous petals shimmering and flowing with all colors of the spectrum. Even the sky was strange. Sometimes boiling clouds hung only inches above their heads, reaching down snaky, greasy tendrils as if trying to grab them. Other times the sky was a tremendous bloodred dome in which no star sparkled, no sun shone, no moon rose. And at all times they walked in uncanny, unnerving stillness.

Finally, after a minute or a week, they were in a forbidding countryside of jagged black rocks that looked like obsidian, or volcanic glass. The path narrowed until it rose to a pass where they would have to go through single file.

"That is the doorway to Nyarlat-Hotep's domain," said Brewster, sounding worried.

"Then," returned the professor, "let us venture forth." He grasped the hilt of his Knights of Columbus sword and led the way on the upward climb.

"HALT!"

The hollow, booming voice made Johnny jump in surprise and alarm. He saw that a figure stood on either side of the narrow pass, like guards. They were immense. Each was at least ten feet tall. Their bodies were vaguely human. They bulged with muscles. The hands and feet were webbed, with cruel red claws. The heads were the most frightening detail. They were those of crocodiles, with long, yellow, grinning teeth bared. Worst of all, their eyes had been sewn shut with zigzags of heavy red cord. From the mutilated eyelids, rivulets of dried blood ran down.

The head of the left guardian swung slowly toward them. "DOOM," it thundered. "DOOM AWAITS HE WHO ENTERS HERE. NONE SHALL PASS!"

The other creature gaped its jaws, its fangs dripping. "NONE SHALL PASS," it echoed.

For a moment the group stood trembling before the two guardians. Then, as if with a sudden inspiration, the professor stepped forward. "I," he said in a high- pitched voice quite unlike his normal tones, "I am Sister Teresa Genevieve."

There was a long, puzzled silence. Then the guardian on the left said, "I BEG YOUR PARDON?"

"I am Sister Teresa Genevieve," repeated the professor. "I am a nun, and you said, 'Nuns shall pass.'"

"DID WE, ALARIC?" asked the guardian on the right.

"THAT'S WHAT WE SAID, ALL RIGHT. SHE'S GOT US, LEO," responded the other one. "RIGHT. ER, IN YOU GO, THEN."

Professor Childermass winked at the others and strode past the unmoving monsters. Fergie whispered, "I'm not even Catholic!"

"Make something up," Johnny whispered back. He said, "I am Sister Mary Frances," in a high, piping voice.

"UH, RIGHT, YOU MAY PASS," said the figure on the left.

Johnny walked through and turned to grin at Fergie.

Fergie made a face at him and in high, mincing tones, he said, "And I am Sister Francine Hildegarde Ursula John Cameron Swayze."

"UH, GO ON IN, THEN," replied the monster.

As Fergie joined them, Brewster soared high over the pass and landed on the path in front of him. He gestured, and the three friends began to climb down the steep path. Behind them, Johnny heard one of the creatures say, "LOT OF NUNS AROUND LATELY. SUPPOSE THERE'S A CONVENTION OR SOMETHING?"

He did not hear the response.

They rounded a sharp curve, and Johnny took a deep breath. Not far ahead, the pathway leveled out. It led across a dismal flat expanse of bare black rock. And in the distance lay a castle straight out of a fever dream. It seemed close, but that was only because of its immensity. Spires rose and sent out shoots that became turrets, towers, and parapets. Walls ascended at crazy angles and lost themselves in a wilderness of obelisks, caryatids, and columns. It looked like the kind of structure that, on earth, a million groaning slaves would have to work on for six hundred years. Its walls were a deep, dusky brown, but not a window looked out of that terrible structure.

"My dad is in there?" asked Johnny, feeling like bawling. "How will we ever find him?"

"You will find him," Brewster assured him in a somber voice. "That won't be the problem. You have to be prepared to—" Suddenly his head snapped around. "Fly!" he screeched, sounding terrified. "Fly! *The minions of Nyarlat-Hotep are upon you!*"

And rising from unseen hiding places all across the plain, dozens of nightmares sprang up howling.

CHAPTER THIRTEEN

To Roderick Childermass, the oncoming army was a body of German soldiers from World War I, gripping their rifles and lowering their heads with their spiked helmets gleaming as they ran. He retreated, trying to find some cover. The sharp cough of a machine gun rattled away to one side. The screams of incoming artillery shells wailed overhead. He scrambled to find shelter.

Then he heard a woman's voice call, "Roderick! Help me, please!"

He gasped and turned, his eyes wide in disbelief. The German soldiers had formed a line. They had raised their rifles. They were pointing them at a slim, beautiful woman who stood in front of a pitted, bullet-riddled wall. "Yvette?" asked the professor. "You're dead!"

"You let them kill me," the woman said in French. "You are a coward! You were always a coward!"

The professor covered his face with trembling hands. He began to sob. "You betrayed me!" he said, his voice muffled. "I thought you were working for our side, and I fell in love with you. You tried to turn me over to the Germans!"

"You ran away!" the woman screamed. "You left me to die in your place! You coward! You despicable coward!"

Professor Childermass gave one wrenching, deep sob. Then he dropped his hands, his eyes streaming tears. "You are not real! You were a German spy, and you died nearly forty years ago!" He drew his Knights of Columbus sword. "Coward, am I? Charge!"

And swinging the sword in a wild arc, he ran right for the astonished line of German soldiers. They jerked their rifles toward him, but too late! He was among them, the sword whistling and screeching as if it had a life of its own! Left and right, he slashed and hacked—

But the sword touched no flesh. The soldiers melted away, becoming mist. Mocking, booming laughter filled the air. Panting, the professor turned to face the woman. She stood straight and tall before the bullet-pocked wall. "Old fool!" she screamed. "Welcome to the Palace of Dreadful Night! You are the captive of Nyarlat-Hotep, the Goat with a Thousand Young!"

"I'll settle your hash, you—you infernal illusion," growled Professor Childermass, rushing toward the figure in white.

Before he got to her, she changed, her features flowing and reforming. Now she was a skeleton, with bones barely concealed by a horrible tight covering of yellow, parchmentlike dried skin. It grinned at him, a taunting red light in the depths of its eye sockets. "Idiot!" it said. "Weakling! You are nothing against me!"

Professor Childermass swung the sword. It passed through the space where the creature had stood not a second before. Now it was just empty air. The sword struck sparks from the wall—

And the professor found himself all alone in the dark. Or had he been struck blind? The darkness was so complete, he could not tell.

Fergie saw them coming for him—a legion of boys bigger and stronger than he was, sneering at him. They wore leather jackets and were pounding their fists into the palms of their hands. "Hey, sissy!" one of them yelled. "Yeah, you! We're gonna pound you good! We're gonna smash you right into th' ground! An' then we're gonna go to your house an' beat up your old man and your mama. How ya like that, baby?"

"You leave them alone!" screamed Fergie in fear and outrage. "You think you're strong enough to fight me? Just come on, you cheap hoods! But leave my folks alone!"

"His dad's a failure," another one said with an evil snicker.

"He worked for th' same comp'ny twenny years an' only got one promotion! An' his mom's a real slob. She—"

"Shut up!" Fergie yelled. "Shut up, you!"

They all laughed at him. The laughter hit him like a million tiny daggers, plunging into him, piercing his defenses, and letting all his courage pour out. He sank to his knees, sobbing.

"Crybaby!" the hoods began to chant as they encircled him. "Crybaby, crybaby!"

Fergie groaned. They were right. He had always tried to act tough, but he was soft inside. And he had been ashamed of his family. When he was little, they had been so poor. And his father was such a meek man, and his mother was so thin and worried all the time—

"It was just a front, huh, tough guy?" asked a snarling voice. Fergie looked up. A skeleton stood in front of him, a skeleton wearing a studded leather jacket. Its face was like that of a mummy, bone beneath a drum-tight layer of withered yellow skin. Its grin was sardonic and evil, and red hatred smoldered in the depths of its hollow eye sockets. "All that athletic ability and all that tough talk. You're nothin' but a sissy, Ferguson! In fact, you're nothin' at all!"

Fergie felt like sinking into the ground. But then, deep inside himself, he found a hot red spark of anger. He concentrated on it, and it burst into flames.

With a wordless roar, Fergie sprang to his feet. "Come on!" he bellowed. "Yah, you talk big, but come on! Let's see whatcha got, you bag o' bones! You think you can take me? Give it a try, baby! Just give it a try!"

With a shout, the hoods leaped at him. Fergie fought back with fists and feet, punching and kicking wildly. None of his blows connected. They went right through his enemies, and they popped like soap bubbles until only the skeleton was left standing. Fergie stood exhausted and panting.

"You are mine," said the skeleton, its mesmerizing, evil smile becoming wider. "I think I shall take away your mind and leave you a thrashing, babbling hulk! Come in, fool! Come into the Palace of Dreadful Night!"

And immediately, Fergie found himself in utter darkness. "Johnny?" he shouted, absolutely terrified. "Professor?"

The endless night swallowed up his words. It swallowed him.

Johnny fled from everything he had ever been afraid of. Enormous insects pursued him, hopping, flopping, moaning, buzzing, their terrible scratchy legs scrabbling the ground. People with their jaws locked open ran bawling after him, trying to infect him with tetanus. Formless things screeched and gibbered, their blobby bodies blossoming with eyes, with gaping mouths, with clutching claws that dissolved immediately.

He was among the endless pillars, towers, and turrets of the castle. He screamed as he ran, feeling ashamed of his own cowardice. But he could not, he could not stand and face those frightful things. Somehow he saw a doorway right in front of him, a high, sharply arched opening. He barreled through it, into the dark.

And there was light.

It was dim, it was pale, and it came from far ahead, but it was blessed, welcome light. Johnny staggered toward it on legs that almost refused to carry him. He could not stop gulping and panting.

He blundered into his father's hospital room.

"Dad!" yelled Johnny.

His father opened his eyes. They were horrible. They were black pools, just like the vision he had seen.

"You let me die," his father said.

Johnny sank to the floor, unable to stand up. "No," he said weakly.

"Yes!" said Major Dixon. "And because you are such a sniveling coward, your grandmother and grandfather will die! And Father Higgins! And Sarah, your friend! And it's all your fault! All yours!"

Johnny could not stand it. He screamed in agony. And then he heard the monstrous, evil laughter.

The figure in the bed stood, and it became the grinning ghost of Damon Boudron. "Fool!" it shouted in triumph. "Pitiful fool! Don't you even realize what has happened? I have your father's soul captive here, in my palace. But he would not surrender to me! So I lured you here—you and those meddling friends of yours! Now they will die, and you will watch as they do. And then I will give your wretched father a simple choice: Bow to me, or watch me torture you to madness, death, and even worse. Which choice will he take, do you think? Will the brave Major Dixon sacrifice himself for his only son? Of course he will! You have given the universe to me, John Dixon! I have won!"

The frightful fiend strode closer and closer. It reached out a bony hand to grasp Johnny's arm. He could stand it no longer. Johnny fainted dead away.

CHAPTER FOURTEEN

"Johnny?"

Johnny opened his eyes. It was his father's voice. But he could see only darkness. "D-Dad?"

The major's voice was unbearably weary: "He told me you were here."

"I c-came to help you, Dad. I'm so s-sorry."

For a long time Johnny was afraid that his father was gone. Then, his tired, tortured voice once more broke the silence: "That's all right, Old Scout."

Johnny lay on a cold stone floor. He pushed himself up and groped with his hands. He had a terror now of tumbling into a deep hole, like the one in Edgar Allan Poe's story "The Pit and the Pendulum." And there were rats in that story too, and red-hot walls. Johnny groaned. Was there nothing that he wasn't afraid of?

"Johnny?"

Another voice, from far away. "P-Professor?"

"Hang on," said the professor's voice. "I've given up cigarettes, but I still have my faithful Nimrod lighter."

A glimmer of light! "I see you!" Johnny yelled. "Dad? Where are you?"

"I don't know," said his father. "I can't move, anyway. You go, Johnny. Get away from this terrible place."

"Not without you," replied Johnny. He struck out for the little spark of light. "I'm coming, Professor," he shouted.

From a long way off, Fergie yelled, "Me too, Prof!"

"Hurry!" called Professor Childermass. "This thing burns fuel like crazy!"

Fergie and Johnny reached the professor at almost the

same instant. The old man let his lighter go out, but in the dark he threw an arm around each boy's shoulders. "I thought we were all goners," he said. "Now where are we? And what's the next step?"

"Prof, where's Brewster?" asked Fergie. "Seems to me we need light right now, an' one of his tricks is to shed light on any situation."

"Brewster!" called Professor Childermass. "Did you hear that?"

A moment later a pink glow surrounded them. Brewster himself was invisible, but his raspy voice said sullenly, "I'm in the soup with you now. Here's your light. Not that I think it will help much!"

Johnny looked around. They seemed to be in a vast cavern, so big that neither walls nor ceiling was visible. The floor they stood on was a dead flat black. Really, all they could see was each other.

"Any suggestions, Brewster?" asked the professor.

"Just one," returned Brewster's voice. "Remember, Nyarlat-Hotep has taken on material form from your world. What is material can be destroyed. But watch out! He will try to terrify you by throwing your worst fears right back at you!"

"Tell me about that," groused Fergie. "So what do we do about it?"

Slowly, Johnny said, "I think we have to get rid of all our fear. We have to concentrate on things that will keep that out of our mind. Things like, well, our friendship. And our families."

"Right you are," said the professor. "Well, kiddies, it's time to find our playmate. Let's go!"

They walked carefully through the darkness, surrounded by a moving pool of pink light provided by Brewster. Before long they came to a double row of pillars, each one about fifteen feet high. They were thin, with Corinthian crowns, and atop each one perched a human skull. The professor counted them. "Twelve," he declared fiercely. "It's plain that this is Boudron's trophy room. These are the remains of his first twelve sacrifices. Let's see what we can do about this."

He shoved at one of the pillars. "Give me—umph!—a little help here, please!"

Johnny and Fergie put their shoulders to the pillar. It was made of what felt like corroded iron. After two hard shoves it fell over, crashing into the next pillar. That one hit the next in line, like a row of dominoes, until six had collapsed with an unholy clatter. Then they overthrew the columns on the right. "Okay," panted Fergie. "What did that do?"

"It made me feel better!" roared the professor. "Now, let's see what is at the top of that stairway!"

"What stairway?" asked Johnny, but then he saw it. Just past the place where the last pillars had toppled, a huge staircase began. The stairs had to be a hundred feet broad, and they climbed up into empty darkness. The three began to ascend.

It seemed to take forever. Johnny's legs felt dead. Finally he stumbled against the professor and realized they were no longer climbing. "Oh, saints of mercy!" muttered the professor. "Don't look, Johnny!"

But it was too late. With a cry of horror, Johnny saw what lay ahead. In a lurid wash of red light, he could see a wall. A wall made up of black stone, with the bones and skulls of human beings embedded in it. And in the center of the red light, like a performer on some gruesome stage, was Johnny's father.

He had become part of that wall. His anguished face showed, and one of his arms. Part of one leg and one foot. His face was cheek by jowl beside a bare skull. Slimy slugs crept over his forehead and his bare arm. His face was seamed with marks of suffering.

"Johnny," he said with a groan. "Go away! Go home!"

Johnny ran forward. He swatted at the loathsome creeping things. "We've come to save you, Dad!" he said.

Evil laughter echoed. The professor and Fergie clustered close to Johnny. They looked all around. Then the professor said, "There you are, you fiend!" He drew his sword and charged.

Johnny whirled. He saw the skeletal form of Damon

Boudron standing at the edge of the red light. The professor took a terrific swashing blow with his Knights of Columbus sword. The ghost held up a bony hand and struck at the swishing blade. With a crack and a clang, the sword broke to pieces.

Professor Childermass staggered, staring at the hilt and its four inches of remaining blade. "Drat!" he said. "That is the second one of these things I have broken!"

The grinning ghost stepped closer, and the old man fell back. "I will reduce you to madness," purred the spook. "I will strike you blind and deaf! I will cause all the indignities and weaknesses of old age to descend on you in one second! And then your body shall die, and your soul shall become my servant!"

Johnny felt electricity in the air. His hair moved as if it were floating. Blue sparks crackled all around him. The ghost was raising its arms, as if about to cast some dire spell.

Then Johnny noticed that Fergie had dropped to all fours. Like a scuttling crab, he hustled to a position behind the walking skeleton. Johnny realized what Fergie was doing. It was an ancient school yard trick!

The professor realized it too. He cowered back, shielding his face with his hands. "No! No! Dreadful apparition, why do you trouble me?" he screeched. "Take the children! Oh, I am so frightened!"

The grisly creature paused, as if puzzled. Its hands, with sparks boiling off them like flashes from a Roman candle, hesitated. "I do not feel your fear," the monster said.

"Feel this!" bellowed the professor, and he gave the walking skeleton a huge shove right in the center of its chest.

With an outraged scream of surprise, the monster stumbled back—and tripped over the crouching Fergie! It clattered to the floor, then leaped up with surprising speed.

"Rolling block, Dixon!" hollered Fergie.

Johnny threw himself to the floor and did a barrel roll into the skeletal legs. For a second time the horrible specter staggered back, snarling. But this time it was at the head of the huge stair. It fell down into darkness.

"Pursue him!" called the voice of Brewster.

He did not need to encourage the three. Yelling like maniacs, they clattered down the stairway, just in time to see the skeleton crash to the floor. In a flash of blue light, the skull rolled off.

"We did it!" shouted Fergie. "We knocked his block off!"

"Look out!" Johnny screamed.

The skeleton had somehow re-formed itself. Except this time it was not a skeleton at all. It was a snarling tiger, crouching to spring!

"Transmigration!" the voice of Brewster screeched. "He must drink the water of Lethe!"

The professor fumbled in his pocket, and Johnny reached for his own corked vial. But the tiger was springing! It struck the professor and bore him down on the stairway, its great jaws open to clamp on the old man's neck!

"No!" cried Johnny. Then he saw the professor's hands jerk convulsively. A flame leaped forward. The old man had pulled not the bottle of water, but his lighter, from his pocket.

The tiger howled as the jet of fire struck its open mouth. It turned its head from the searing heat. With a stench of burning hair, its fur began to blaze, and it leaped away from the professor, clawing at its face.

Fergie danced around the creature, holding his bottle of water. The tiger's fur seemed to catch fire like tinder. Leaping, billowing flames enveloped it. Fergie darted forward, but a sudden vicious swipe of a burning paw hit him, sending him sprawling. His bottle of water shattered off into the darkness.

The tiger threw its head back and howled. Then it collapsed, with a surge of fire and black smoke!

"Not yet!" said Brewster. "It isn't dead! It's changing form!"

The charred body of the tiger burst apart, and from it crawled a horror. Johnny's mind whirled. He felt faint.

A scorpion scuttled toward him—a scorpion at least two feet long, its curved, deadly tail glistening in the light from the still-burning remains of the tiger. A drop of poison hung on the tip of that sting. With fatal purpose, the monstrous creature headed straight for Johnny. Its lobsterlike pincers snapped furiously. Johnny backed away, tripped, and fell on his back. He felt the legs of the scorpion gripping his jeans, felt the weight of the thing clambering up his chest, saw the quivering sting rise to strike—

Slash! The professor swung the sword hilt, with its few remaining inches of blade! The steel snicked through the tail, and the poisonous sting spun away, cut clean off! Johnny cried out in disgust as the bleeding stump of the tail stabbed with impotent fury against his cheek and throat.

Fergie had crawled to help. He stuck his hand beneath the nasty body and flipped it off Johnny's chest. "You're nothin' but a bug now!" he bellowed. "An' Byron Q. Ferguson steps on bugs!"

The scorpion's thrashing body landed—splat!—on the stone, and true to his word, Fergie staggered up, leaped, and landed with both feet right in the center of the thing's back. With a sickening crack and splurt, the enormous arachnid body burst apart.

"The water!" screeched Brewster from somewhere in the darkness. "You must use the water!"

"On what?" asked Fergie, looking at the runny, burst ruin of the scorpion.

"There!" yelled Professor Childermass. "I see something dark—it's scuttling away!"

A black shape swooped down from the air, a beak stabbed downward, and suddenly the form of Brewster stood before them, clutching something in the tip of his beak. "The water!" he bawled.

A high, insectlike voice shrieked, "You dare not! You cannot! I command you! I, Nyarlat-Hotep, call my minions!"

With shaking hands Johnny pulled his own vial of Lethe water from his pocket. He popped out the cork. In the darkness all around, he heard snarls, growls, and howls. Awful creatures were coming! He could smell their foul breath, could hear the scrape of misshapen hooves and claws on the stone—

"For Dad!" he shouted. "The water of Lethe!"

Brewster took a birdlike hop toward him and held out his beak. "Here! Hold it still!"

The insect voice screamed, "No! *Nooooo!*"

Brewster opened his beak, and something small dropped into the bottle. "Cork!"

Johnny jammed the cork in. Pandemonium howled all around.

Fergie grabbed the vial. "Shake well!" he said, and he shook the vial so vigorously that Johnny couldn't even see it. It was just a blur.

The sounds grew to an unbearable pitch. The professor sank to his knees, his hands pressed over his ears. Johnny ground his teeth together. Fergie staggered—

Then an awful hush fell.

And the world began to melt.

"Dad!" shouted Johnny.

"He's not here!" Brewster said. "Follow me!"

Light ahead. They ran, crawled, stumbled toward it! And then somehow they were on the gray plain, and they had the impression of vast forms fleeing on all sides, sinking into the ground, soaring into the heavens, their wails fading, fading.

The Palace of Dreadful Night flowed, twisted, shrieked as it collapsed. As its great form toppled toward them, Johnny began to scream out an Our Father. He was sure he would die in the next second.

But then the falling mass faded to vapor. The vapor trailed away.

"And leave not a wrack behind," said the professor, his voice shaky. "Did the water work?"

"Pour it out," suggested Brewster.

Fergie uncorked the vial and emptied the water on the ground. A small black shape lay curled in a ball for a moment. Then it straightened and painfully crawled away.

"An ant?" asked Fergie.

"Just an ant," said Brewster. "An ant with no memory

of having been Damon Boudron or a grinning ghost or Nyarlat-Hotep. An ant that starts now to work its way back up to something that might one day, in a million years or so, have a dim kind of thought in its head." After a moment Brewster coughed. "I'll try to watch over him from now on and keep him out of mischief. He *is* my brother."

"Where's Dad?" asked Johnny.

Brewster bowed his head. "His spirit was released at the same time you heard the others go," he said. "It has returned to earth, to his body. But it is not whole. The things Nyarlat-Hotep did to him here will have broken your father's mind. Unless help comes, he will be insane for the rest of his life."

Johnny began to cry. He could not help it.

"I'm sorry," said Brewster. "I am so sorry."

CHAPTER FIFTEEN

D r. Coote and Father Higgins were frantic. Their friends had vanished, along with the book that was their gateway to the strange world of the spirits. How could they get them back?

Biting his lip, Dr. Coote said, "Father Higgins, you say the most powerful prayers you know. I will recite an ancient magic ritual that is supposed to call spirits from the vasty deep."

"But will they come when you do call them?" asked Father Higgins with a grimace. "Very well. I have no idea of anything else that might help, so let's try it."

For fifteen minutes, they did. And then something happened: The air shimmered with a lovely, pearly radiance. A fog formed. And when it dissolved, there stood Johnny, Fergie, and the professor, looking much the worse for wear. They were exhausted, muddy, weeping, scratched, and bruised, but they were all alive.

"We have to get to the hospital!" said Professor Childermass. "And on the double!"

They all piled into Father Higgins's big Oldsmobile, and he drove them to the hospital, running every stoplight along the way. Father Higgins pulled the car up on the sidewalk right in front of the doors, and they climbed out and rushed inside.

Johnny skidded to a halt. He saw his grandfather ahead of him, and he looked terrible, his face a mask of anguish. "Grampa!" yelled Johnny. "Grampa, is Dad—"

His grandfather hugged him. "Oh, Johnny, it's awful! He came to, but he's screamin' and screamin' like a crazy person! He doesn't recognize us, an' he thinks horrible monsters are after him!"

The professor and the others looked at each other with helpless frustration. "Can I see him?" asked Johnny.

His grandfather burst into tears. "No, Johnny, he wouldn't want you to see him like this. It's better if y' don't. The doctors gave Kate a shot to calm her down, an' they're tryin' to get some sedatives into Harrison too, but—"

Professor Childermass put his hand on Grampa's shoulder. "Henry," he said, "let's at least go up to the waiting room."

They did. Praying, comforting each other, or just sitting quietly, they waited for hours. From the room down the hall, they could hear horrible sounds, the sounds of Major Dixon's shrieks and screams and pleas for mercy. At last the professor went down the hall, peeked in the room, and then walked into a stairwell. He put his hand to his face. "Brewster," he said. "Brewster, are you there?"

"Here," came the raspy voice.

"For God's sake, do something," pleaded the professor. "We saved your world. You can at least help us now."

"I can't," said Brewster, sounding as if he too were on the verge of tears. "I would if I could, but I simply cannot. What you ask is beyond human help, and beyond mine. I am so sorry."

The professor stood there, feeling angrier and angrier. It wasn't fair! Johnny had risked his life—had risked more than his life. It just wasn't fair at all!

He heard slow footsteps climbing toward him. With his blood pressure and his anger rising, he drew himself up. He would tell off whoever this was, but good! It might not help, but it would make him feel better.

But then an old woman climbed into view. The professor's jaw dropped. "Madam Lumiere?" he asked.

She gave him a weak, tired smile. "We have all been busy," she said. She came to his level and stood a few steps away from him. "One drop," she said. "One drop in a thousand drops. And then one drop of that. To forget is to heal. To heal is to forget."

"Wh-what?" asked the professor.

"One drop of one drop in a thousand drops," whispered the old woman. And then she began to glow.

The professor almost dropped to his knees in astonishment. The old woman stood straight. Pure light streamed out of her. The years fell away, and she became an unearthly creature, womanlike, but not like any living woman. She had a proud, disdainful face, a face that was ageless. She was cold and bright and beautiful. And her beauty was terrible. She gave him a smile—and he could not tell whether it was a smile of cruelty or of compassion. She seemed far beyond such human feelings.

Trembling in every limb, the professor watched the form of light drift upward, to the ceiling, *through* the ceiling. And the light faded, and he stood alone. "What the devil?" he asked himself. And then he shook his head. "No," he said aloud. "I should not have mentioned the devil. Hmm. A thousand drops. One drop. I wonder—"

He took out his vial of Lethe water. He went back into the hospital and into a patient's room. The patient, a young man, was fast asleep. The professor picked up a water glass, filled it to the brim from a pitcher of ice water, and then, very carefully, allowed one tiny drop of the Lethe water to fall into it.

Then he found an eyedropper and used it first to stir the water and then to take one drop from the glass. "If this doesn't work," he muttered, dumping the rest of the water down the drain, "I am going to swallow the drops of Lethe water in that vial myself! I'd rather know nothing at all than spend the rest of my life knowing I'd failed my friends!"

He pushed into the major's room. The doctors had strapped Major Dixon to the bed, but he still strained and jerked at his bindings. A physician looked up. "You can't come in here," he said. "The sedatives haven't worked, and—"

The professor winced. The major's head was thrown back, and from his open mouth issued a horrible animal scream. With one step the professor was beside the bed. In a quick movement he let the drop of water fall into the major's open mouth. "Let me know if there's any change," he said, hurrying out into the hall.

But the doctor didn't need to come after him. The major's

terrible scream died away. Through the closed door, the professor could hear the major saying, "Johnny? Where's my son?"

He ran down the hallway to the waiting room. Like an elderly shepherd, he moved them down the hall, all of them: Dr. Coote, Father Higgins, Fergie, Henry Dixon, and Johnny.

A smiling doctor opened the major's room door. Johnny plunged past him. "Dad!"

"Johnny!" said Major Dixon, his voice weak but full of joy. "Old Scout! I've been having such nightmares—but I can't even remember them now!"

Everyone clustered around the bed, laughing joyfully. The professor, who hated to let anyone see him cry, quietly left. He walked downstairs. He stepped outside and stood there harrumphing and polishing his spectacles.

To his surprise, the eastern sky was growing pale. He looked at his pocket watch. The night had been longer than he thought. Sunrise was on its way. He chuckled to himself. Tomorrow was the first of July. Sarah would be back, and what a story Johnny would have to tell her. And now maybe Harrison Dixon would get it through his thick head that it was time to retire from the Air Force. Why, he could buy that nice little cottage just down the street from Henry and Kate. He and Johnny could be father and son full-time, not just when the major was on leave.

A dark shape swooped from the sky. "Whatcha doin', Whiskers?"

The professor laughed. "Daydreaming, you flying turkey. We humans do it sometimes."

"Yeah? So do we gods of Upper and Lower Egypt," said Brewster. And he shot straight upward, his falcon's wings spread wide to welcome the brilliant light of a beautiful new day.

ABOUT THE AUTHOR

John Bellairs is beloved as a master of Gothic young adult novels and fantasies. His series about the adventures of Lewis Barnavelt and his uncle Jonathan, which includes *The House with a Clock in Its Walls*, is a classic. He also wrote a series of novels featuring the character Johnny Dixon. Among the titles in that series are *The Curse of the Blue Figurine*; *The Mummy, The Will, and The Crypt*; *The Spell of the Sorcerer's Skull*; and others. His solo novel *The Face in the Frost* is also regarded as a fantasy classic, and among his earlier works are *St. Fidgeta and Other Parodies* and *The Pedant and the Shuffly*.

Bellairs was a prolific writer, publishing more than one dozen novels before his untimely death in 1991.

Brad Strickland has written and cowritten forty-one novels, many of them for younger readers. He is the author of the fantasy trilogy *Moon Dreams, Nul's Quest*, and *Wizard's Mole*, and the creator of the popular horror novel *Shadowshow*. With his wife, Barbara, he has written for the Star Trek Young Adult book series, for Nickelodeon's *Are You Afraid of the Dark?* book series, and for *Sabrina, the Teenage Witch* (Pocket Books). Both solo and with Thomas E. Fuller, he has written several books about Wishbone, public TV's literature-loving dog. When he's not writing, he teaches English at Gainesville College in Gainesville, Georgia. He and Barbara have two children, Amy and Jonathan, and a daughter-in-law, Rebecca. They live and work in Oakwood, Georgia.

OPEN ROAD

INTEGRATED MEDIA

Open Road Integrated Media is a digital publisher and multimedia content company. Open Road creates connections between authors and their audiences by marketing its ebooks through a new proprietary online platform, which uses premium video content and social media.

CPSIA information can be obtained
at www.ICGtesting.com
Printed in the USA
BVOW11s2224190217
476598BV00001B/13/P